JEZEBEL

A Coming-Of-Age Novel

Lesley Meirovitz Waite

Manasa Press

This book is a work of fiction. Names, characters, places, and incidents are either the product of the author's imagination or are used fictitiously. Any resemblance to actual persons, living or dead, events or locales is entirely coincidental.

Book Design and Layout: Baz Here and Casey Waite

ISBN: 979-8-218-19190-0
Printed in the United States of America

Manasa Press
Brooklyn, NY
lesleymwaite.com

"But the Emperor has nothing on at all!" said a little child.

"Listen to the voice of innocence!" exclaimed her father; and what the child had said was whispered from one to another.

"But he has on nothing at all!" at last cried out all the people. The Emperor was vexed, for he felt that the people were right; but he thought the procession must go on now. And the lords of the bedchamber took greater pains than ever to appear holding up a train, although, in reality, there was no train to hold.

-The Emperor's New Clothes,
Andersen's Fairy Tales by *Hans Christian Anderson*

Also by Lesley Meirovitz Waite

Walking On Train Tracks

CONTENTS

CHAPTER ONE: WAIT FOR ME

Jerry's Diner on Beacon was, as its sign said, *Best Eatery in Boston* 1960-1974. Pictures on the window advertised chicken in a basket, fish and chips, thick steak, with the words *Great Place for Family Dinner*! in neon letters above the door. Jerry stood out front greeting people, his black hair slicked back, sports jacket open, bright white teeth flashing. Dad shook his hand and Jerry led us to a big table with a 'reserved' sign which he whisked away. The smells of hamburger, fries, and their famous Boston Cream Pie made my stomach growl.

It was a muggy June evening, the end of junior year for me. My sister Rachel had just graduated high school and both of us were reluctant for this dinner. My best friend Amy had invited me for a sleep-over with friends including my sometimes boyfriend Eric and everyone would be there before we scattered for the summer. Rachel was going to Jacob's Pillow in the Berkshires for a summer internship and was already weepy about missing her boyfriend. I was weepy about Rachel going away all summer for this internship and soon after, college! Me alone in the house with my parents. Ugh.

And mostly, our family dinners seldom ended well.

Except, Mom had insisted.

Rachel and I ordered our usual fare—crisp and chewy fried chicken, well-done fries and coleslaw with Tab to drink. Mom ordered flounder with a Long Island Iced Tea, and Dad ordered a steak and a beer. Drinks came and Mom sucked hers down. When the food arrived she ordered another—her eyes were glassy and her words slurred—she was skinny and didn't have a lot of tolerance for booze.

"You don't need another," Dad said after the waiter was gone.

Dad was handsome with short, thick light brown hair, even brows, sad brown eyes, a strong jaw, and a crooked nose that had been broken many times from being Jewish and fighting with the Boston Irish Catholic boys in high school. Mom was Jewish and British, beautiful, especially when she smiled, with black hair, blue eyes, with a small upright nose which she said helped her pass for non-Jewish when it mattered, during war time in England. People said she had a great figure which I interpreted as big boobs, a thin waist and shapely legs. She always wore stylish dresses and didn't like garish jewelry, flashy clothes, or loud women. Very specific opinions, Mom had.

She ignored Dad's comment about the drink. "Tell us all about your internship, Rachel sweetheart, do I need to get your tutu dry cleaned, your tap shoes polished?" Mom lit a cigarette, tilted her head and smiled at her own charm.

"I told you, this summer is modern dance and jazz, remember? We talked about it a hundred times." Rachel stole a glance my way.

I whispered in her ear, "Don't go, Rachel. Be at the beach house with me like always. I don't want to be alone with them."

"It'll be okay, Jez," she said, and patted me on the knee.

It wouldn't be okay, I knew it. Every summer we'd go to our beach house on the South Shore and Rachel was part of my gang. She was *always* there.

Rachel asked Dad about driving her to the Berkshires and I perused the other tables—couples with their heads close, families looking normal and laughing, talking, relaxed. Mom's second drink came and no one said anything as she stamped out her cigarette in her barely eaten fish, with the sizzle of ash against butter and lemon juice. A wasted meal which I was about to stick my fork into.

"Mom, that was good fish. Why'd you ruin it?"

She flicked her hair back. "Oh Jezebel, it's only fish, and you've had enough. You can pick the movie if you're upset about the fish."

Movie? There was no way. I nudged Rachel with my knee and shook my head, secret language, but she didn't look at me. She pulled her pink sweater with the yellow butterflies over her yellow mini-dress. Rachel had long blond hair which was usually in a bun, tall at 5'8 to my 5'6 with a lean dancer's body to my athletic, curvier one. Blue eyes to my brown ones. She was eighteen and I would be seventeen in October and our personalities were really different. She ignored stuff with our parents, whereas I wanted to point everything out. We never spoke about Mom's drinking. Once I had attempted and she said it was nothing, Mom was just having fun and not to be so serious. When I told her about the thing with Dad, she said the same thing.

"No movie tonight, Sylvia," Dad said. "I'm tired."

Spilled Tab made a blot next to my plate with some fried chicken crust on the outer edge of its circle. I stuck my finger in it and made a pattern, like mountains.

Jerry came over and stood between my parents, smiling and glancing around the table. "How was everything, Saul?" Dad was in real estate and knew a lot of the restaurant owners from golf and business.

"Great, as usual." Dad pushed back his chair. "Good joint you're running, Jerry."

The smoke from Mom's cigarette twirled a hazy pattern in the dim light. She batted her eyes and sucked in her cheeks. "Jerry, you can settle this for us. We're going to the movies, any suggestions?" Her British accent was especially thick around men.

"Blazing Saddles is good, very funny." Jerry nodded like he was going to leave and Mom said, her voice high and flirty, "Oh, we saw that, all the farting around the campfire," and she actually made dainty farting noises, "Pffft, pffft."

Rachel and I stared at each other, horrified, as hysterical laughter threatened to overtake me. I couldn't even look at Mom, with her lips, cheekbones, eyelashes, totally unaware. Dad rose to shake Jerry's hand, both men ignoring Mom's comment, and in that silent language men have, a look was exchanged. I saw it. What did it mean? Pay no attention, Jerry, she's had too much to drink, or, it's okay, Saul, my wife says stupid things all the time, see you on the golf course, we'll have a cigar, talk business. Mom was still looking at Jerry and a heat ran through me. I felt embarrassed for her, and a mixture of other things I couldn't explain. Things that burned inside making me want to disappear.

At the next table a huge piece of cake was placed in front of a boy with red hair as his family, waiters, and soon most of the restaurant sang Happy Birthday. His family was smiling, candles flickered before him as he closed his eyes for the wish and blew them out as everyone applauded.

What did he wish for? A new bike? To win his next baseball game? To become invisible?

Dad added up the check and placed a twenty on the table. "Let's go." He reached for his navy-blue sport jacket.

Rachel pushed back her chair. "Come on, Mom."

Mom wasn't moving. "How about Alice Doesn't Live Here Anymore, or a nice family car ride?"

"That movie's not out yet, Mom," Rachel said, with a plea to her voice that I knew said, let's not make a scene.

Dad stood up and Mom glared at him. "We never go anywhere— you'll just watch TV and what will I do? Sit there and read a book? Stare into space?" Her voice was getting whiny with sharp edges, Dad was tired from the stress of building his business and Rachel and I definitely did not want to witness another fight. Everyone seemed to be looking at us as Dad's voice grew louder.

"Not tonight, Sylvie. I'm tired and the kids want to be with their friends. We're going home."

Mom sipped the remnants of her drink which was watery, the ice melted. Anger and pity towards her rose in me mixed with a desire to make her feel better which was futile, it always came back to this. Taking Mom's arm, Dad led her out, Rachel and I following. I glared around at the restaurant. No one noticed us except Jerry who nodded at my dad. At that moment I hated everyone.

As we walked to the car, Mom's complaints continued. Lagging behind, I noticed there were no stars out, the sky pitch black and the sidewalks empty. I wished it would pour big, cold drops and wash away Mom's mood. A dark, beautiful alley was on my left. Cool air blew fresh and I searched for images to cling to—an alley cat, garbage cans, a bottom floor kitchen window with someone playing solitaire in dim light, anything to be lifted away from this tension. Any minute, Dad would erupt into rage because Mom wouldn't stop until that happened.

We walked past another alley with cobblestones. Shadows danced on the building walls and I heard the hum of a harmonica, a soulful tear of notes piercing the air. Two hippie guys sauntered down the alley, swinging their arms, loose, a beat to their step. They wore cowboy boots, jeans, leather fringe. One played the harmonica, an echo of slow, thick notes, creating a rainbow of adventure which beckoned me. I stopped. Watched them. Wanted to follow. I imagined them saying, 'Come with us, Jezebel!' I would nod and say, 'Yes, you are what I've been seeking, your cabin in Vermont near a river, me playing piano in your band, we'll be connected in love, forever, hold on, wait for me...'

My father's harsh voice, "Jezebel. Come on."

The hippies stopped, paused, turned, looked at me and smiled. One held out his hand, welcome to our freedom. Rachel ran back to me and grabbed my arm, "What are you doing? Dad's already mad!" And I was pulled away, their image plastered on my brain. I will find you.

We sat in the car with the engine on. Mom kept talking about a movie. A loud police siren whizzed by, a group of college students spilled out of a building, laughing. Smells of a barbecue, sweet and smoky, crept into my open window.

"Enough!" Dad screamed, the car reverberating.

It seemed there was too little air in the backseat of that Ninety-Eight Oldsmobile. All molecules were thick with Mom's perfume, Dad's frustration, Mom's cigarettes, Dad's rage, Mom's complaints, Dad's excuses and soon his silence which was louder than anything.

Last month at school a student teacher with long hair and a guitar had given me a book, *The Prophet* by Kahlil Gibran, which I carried everywhere, reading a line here and there. It was at my feet and I reached for the book and read aloud. "You were born together, and together you shall be forever more. You shall be together when the white wings of death scatter your days. Ay, you shall be together even in the silent memory of God."

There was dead silence.

Dad's voice exploded, directed at me and the world. "What is that religious crap you are reading Jezebel, white wings of death bullshit, memory of God." He pulled away from the curb, swerving from a car that blasted the horn. Turning from the front seat, Mom faced me, her mouth in a tight line, eyes filled with disgust. Rachel pinched my leg hard, her eyes wide as she shook her head.

The book shifted in my lap. The page I had read was titled 'marriage'. I liked what the author had written, the concept was soothing. As we drove, everyone quiet, collapsed, something started growing inside me. The hippies, their music, their freedom. Was that a sign for my escape? The thought pressed on my insides.

Dad pulled into the driveway and Rachel nudged me out.

In the house, everyone went their separate ways. Mom hurried to mix herself a drink, Rachel and I went into our room, Dad went downstairs. Rachel stuck her nose in a book and we didn't mention the fight since we never talked about them—our unwritten code. "There's nothing we can do," Rachel had said more than once. Maybe not, just, it would be nice to be able to talk about things, dissect them, see even a small thimble of light.

What was that song the hippie played in the alley? Something bluesy. Dad was in the den with the TV low, our piano was in the playroom and I tiptoed past him. On the music rack a songbook was open. Crosby, Stills, Nash and Young. Placing my hands on the smooth keys, I relaxed and played *Wooden Ships*, a song about senseless war and nuclear destruction. About being led away to a more peaceful, happy place.

Yes, exactly what I wanted. Lead me away. Let me laugh.

At the end of the song I just sat and listened. Hum of electricity. Ice cubes tinkled in a glass. Light footsteps and the slide of the porch door as Mom went with her drink to her space, a closed-in porch that no one else used. The rest of the house had settled into dreamers and forgetters.

Lost in the music, I stared at the language of notes, one two three four rest, four four time, beat beat, rest. Images floated in my brain. A Parisian bistro, smoky clubs in Boston, a Cambridge speakeasy.

"Requests anyone?" I said aloud.

Music made me feel something great, something wonderful. Become a musician, tour the world, enter realms of lyrics and melodies, be free, be carried away down an alley, into a dance, a song, possibility. Music was full of heart, pure and true, unlike this house full of lies.

This would be my plan for the summer while Rachel was away. I'd practice the piano. My fake ID would be coming in the mail soon. There was a ferry that went right from our beach house town to Boston. I'd go to the clubs, listen, nod my head, and learn.

Before I went to bed I wrote a letter.

June 21, 1974

TO: Boston Globe, Advice Column

Dear Abby,

I hope you can help me. My family is really messed up. Mom drinks too much and gets sad and sloppy. Dad and Mom scream at each other constantly. And Dad did something that I can't even say. I told my sister and she didn't believe me and pretended nothing was wrong. I'm sixteen and want to run away—my ex-boyfriend is going cross country to California, seeing all the Grateful Dead concerts along the way and he invited me. I really want to go but if I went my Dad would find me and beat the s--- out of me.

It's all so messed up.

Abby, please help. What should I do?

Signed, JB

CHAPTER TWO: BUBBIE IN COOLIDGE CORNER

Two days later, my best friend Amy and I hung out. It was New England June weather, warm one day, cool the next, and I dressed in hip hugger jeans with patched knees, a green tee that a guy from a bar gave me with a picture of a fishing pole that said, 'Jed's Bait', my batik bag, and red converse sneakers. Rachel was at her dance class and I peeked in her drawer looking for money. Her drawer was neat, pencils and pens organized, loose change in a small wooden container, with an actual jewelry box which held her earrings, bracelets and necklaces, all with their own special section. My drawer was a clump of everything, impossible to find anything.

Telling myself I'd replace it at a later date, I grabbed two dollars from her stash. In my drawer, I searched for a brown glass bottle my friend Missy had given me last week in school. Her father was a psychiatrist and he had bottles of crossroads, otherwise known as amphetamines, so many that he didn't notice he supplied Missy and some of her friends. What I wanted this time by taking them was confidence, energy, and especially ideas about where to find jazz piano lessons. I swallowed three small white pills and put two more in my pocket.

I met Amy at the Newton Centre T stop and we hopped on the train.

"We leave next Sunday for Maine," Amy said.

"We leave Saturday for our beach house," I said. We were above ground passing Chestnut Hill reservoir, a place that friends and I walked around when we wanted a woodsy experience that was near our houses. "Hey, let's go to the reservoir when we all get back from the summer," I said, nodding my head towards the water. There was a feeling that came over me of missing Amy already, even though summer had just started.

Today the bright sun reflected off the water, the flowers colorful by the gate that we jumped over when it was locked.

"Sure," Amy said. "But today let's do George's Folly then Boston Common. I have to get some stuff for Maine." Amy adjusted her purse. I always thought she knew more about being a girl than I did; she actually had different colored purses to match all her outfits. Amy had thick blonde red hair that was always brushed neatly; she didn't have clumps of impossible knots like me. She had blue eyes and a wide face—I didn't think she was that pretty but she was so nice and friendly. And mostly, she never looked at me weird like some other girls did. Like my boobs were sticking out or I was wearing a slutty outfit. Amy always smiled at me. Like now.

"So, Jez, what's up with Eric?" Amy said.

"Hmmm," I said. Eric was my boyfriend the past two years and even though he was two years older and at college, we still hung out when he was around. He was European-style handsome, Jewish, with a long nose, curly thick black hair, dark skin over a tight, muscular perfect-for-me body. Eric was the first boy I had sex with and the first one that loved me. Since he went off to college we both went out with other people, and I acted agreeable with this arrangement yet felt some sense of ownership.

"Not sure. He'll visit me at the beach next week. You know..." It was hard to explain these things and Amy didn't press.

Two quick stops and we jumped off at Beacon Street. Business people in suits were having lunch at a sidewalk café and one lady in a hat gave me a sharp look. Was it the rip in my tee or the little braids on the side of my head?

"Amy do I look bad? That lady eye-knifed me."

Amy laughed and hugged me. "You look great. Come on, she's wearing a Queen Elizabeth hat, don't care about her!" We ran across the street.

George's Folly was on the corner. It was my favorite store, selling second hand clothes, bongs, witch-craft books, jewelry, and all-flavored candy sticks at the counter. The owner George sat high up on his throne by the register and greeted people. There was always incense burning and sitar music playing. As we entered through the beaded curtain he waved, and I went to the book section next to the jewelry section while Amy looked at earrings.

A thin book with a bright red cover caught my eye. It was called *Truth and Lies: Historic Feminists*. Amy was in the next aisle and held up a pair of gaudy turquoise earrings.

"Ugly," I said. She nodded, put them back and kept searching.

Flipping through the book my attention landed on a picture of a woman with dark brown skin, long hair and a crown. A caption said in bold letters: *QUEEN JEZEBEL*. My heart started fluttering. I had never seen a picture of her before. She was alluring and there was magic blazing from her eyes.

How I got my name was a bedtime story Mom told me when I was young. A beautiful, French painting teacher in England had given Mom lessons when she was a teenager, which was a real novelty since Mom was poor. The teacher's name was Jezebel, and even though Mom heard from her religious friend Millie that Jezebel was an evil character in the bible, her teacher Jezebel said that Jezebel was in fact a warrior, a defender of the downtrodden, and that people persecuted her because she prayed to different Gods and Goddesses. Since Mom was a minority, a British Jew at the time of World War II, the idea of Jezebel as a patron saint of the oppressed appealed to her and that's why she named me Jezebel.

That description appealed to me, too. Sometimes I felt downtrodden. And I noticed oppressed people all over the place, like the man at the Newton Highlands trolley station with no legs. I think Mom was a bit in love with this French painting teacher. And with the handsome war photographer she always talked about. And a sprinkling of others.

The author in this book described Jezebel like my Mom's teacher had, except they also said she was an actual queen and something else that I really liked—Jezebel was an ambassador to the truth.

Ambassador to the truth. Like me. My Dear Abby letter yesterday.

As I gazed at her picture, something hopeful moved inside me.

"Hey, Amy, there's a picture of me in this book."

Amy came over and I pointed to the photo. "Queen Jezebel. We look alike, don't you think?" I held the book up to my face and made my eyes big and blazing.

Amy laughed. "Nice try."

"She was cool, do you know about her?"

"Sure, Jezebel from the bible. She lied, cheated, stole, was a prostitute and killed some prophets. And she was eaten by dogs."

"That's not true! Listen." I read, "Queen Jezebel was created by misogynists to discredit strong powerful women who enjoyed sex and were better suited as leaders than their husbands. Jezebel was married to a weak king and she killed false prophets so women prophets had power. She played the flute and danced as worship. Jezebel was wise, out-spoken, independent and beautiful, with a strong body, long red hair and dark skin."

Amy shook her head and looked at the cover. "Who wrote that book? That's feminist crap, and the bible is religious c rap, all of it made-up." Amy was into sciences and liked cold, hard facts.

A pause in me as the picture of Jezebel challenged me, her eyes holding a question, *who are you?* She was a musician, like I wanted to become, an outspoken truth teller, like me, she was treated as a foreigner, like I felt in my own family—when I told the truth they acted like there was something wrong with me, something broken and unfixable.

I put the book back and looked at two more books, *The Psychedelic Experience,* about philosophy and LSD, by Dr. Timothy Leary, a prominent Harvard psychologist, and *Meditation*, a compilation of thoughts and instructions about meditation. Amy held up a small turquoise ring, silver with reddish stones surrounding the turquoise. I nodded and we walked to the register where she bought the ring and three cherry sticks for $4.75, and I bought the two books and three black licorice sticks for $3.50. As we walked to the T I felt happy, connected to some inner power. Or maybe the speed was kicking in.

On the train, Amy looked through my books while I thought about dying my hair red, like Queen Jezebel. We both had thick hair even though mine was shoulder-length, and in summer I got as dark as she was. I forgot what color her eyes were but they were probably brown, like mine.

A few stops later we emerged from the train at Boston Common and bells and chanting filled the air. The Hare Krishnas were here. They had recently appeared all over town—Logan Airport, Commonwealth Ave., Copley Square, Cambridge Commons, and I loved how free and happy they were. Six of them were by the grass and we watched as they danced, played hand cymbals and chanted, with one man playing a small wooden boxy piano that had a pump. Men's heads were shaved except for ponytails that were different lengths and colors. Two women had colorful scarves over long hair and orange flowing robes.

A cute Hare Krishna with a blond ponytail and blazing blue eyes, not much older than us, approached holding a book. I glanced at its title: *Science of Self-realization.*

I reached for it and Amy slapped my hand away. "Don't touch it!"

My eyebrows raised as the boy kept smiling. "Do you want a free vegetarian meal?"

I was about to say yes when Amy grabbed my arm and we ran off, laughing.

"Wait, why'd you do that? I wanted the book, and he was cute!" We caught our breath and walked towards the duck pond.

"Once you touch their book, they make you take it, after that they want money, and, you know…it's hard to get away."

I didn't know if I wanted to get away. They seemed so happy, dancing and chanting, 'Hare Krishna, Hare Rama'. "Maybe I'll join!"

Amy laughed. "Your dad would find you and beat the crap out of you."

I reached for a licorice stick and stuck the spicy, sweet candy in my mouth. "That's true. What should we do next?"

Amy sucked her cherry stick and we walked through the common. "I don't know, what should we do?"

A group of toddlers walked by holding hands with two adult leaders in front and two in back. They had slow, short steps, with their hair blowing in the breeze, wearing colorful shirts, probably a summer camp. They seemed too young for camp, a confused, sad march to the swan boats without their parents.

"Let's walk to Copley, Amy, see who's playing at Jazz Workshop. Too bad we're both leaving for the summer, we could club hop together. I'm in search of a jazz piano teacher, not like Mr. Peanut Breath, my old teacher. I mean he was okay, he taught me classical and how to read music, but now I'm all about jazz and blues. Maybe we can go before you take off to Maine?"

Amy raised her eyebrows. "You're talking so fast. Did you do speed?"

My face heated up and I shrugged. "Just a little," I mumbled. Amy wouldn't hold it against me, I knew, just, she was so good and clean, with her pulled back hair and clear eyes.

We walked past a fountain, and a girl with a puppy on a rope who was asking for spare change caught my attention. She appeared so innocent, with long, greasy blond hair that was limp with clumps of dirt, a wilted flower behind her ear. Her face had a few scratches and was dirty, her eyes were a dullish yellow-brown, she was probably pretty at one time and still could be if she cleaned up a bit. The flip-flops she wore were old, one held together with thick black tape.

Her voice was soft. "My puppy's friendly, he doesn't bite. Can you spare any change?"

There was a quarter in my jeans pocket which I gave her. Amy gave her a whole dollar, and the girls' eyes lit up, as well as dull eyes could. "Hey, thanks, what are your names, maybe I'll see you around?"

Amy stuck out her hand which the girl didn't shake. "I'm Amy."

"Jezebel," I said.

"Queen Jezebel," Amy said, laughing.

The girl stuffed the money in her front pocket, the dollar sticking out of a small hole. "My puppy is James Joyce and I'm Daisy," she said, and turned and headed into whatever corner of the city they had emerged from. I imagined she stayed at a commune in Cambridge, or a single-parent apartment in Southie. Maybe at the tent-city by the tracks.

An impulse to stop her, ask, do you have a place to stay, want to sleep on my nice warm carpet, are you okay? But she was quick, gone amongst the Sunday crowds. Daisy made me think of Grandma Bubbie who was a socialist and used to take people into her one bedroom apartment in Dorchester after my parents moved out. Bubbie helped poor people even though she was poor most of her life, until my Dad started his business. Now she lived in a nice neighborhood in Brookline at Coolidge Corner. We didn't see her often, though. Mom didn't get along with her, said it was Bubbie's fault, that when Mom and Dad lived with her in Dorchester before kids, when they were all poor, Bubbie was overpowering.

"Jez, I should go. I have to pack for Maine."

The speed was making me hyper. "Okay, maybe I'll go buy that book about Queen Jezebel at George's Folly. Or visit my grandma Bubbie. Or go see that cute Krishna boy."

I still felt the way that boy looked at me, into my eyes, real, as if he was there. It was alluring and I wanted his book, his offer for food, to visit their run-down house somewhere in Somerville where they had an organic garden with nasty looking vegetables, their kitchen abundant full of apples with bruises and loaves of whole grain bread. I wanted to have sex with that Krishna boy and curl up, he'd chant in my ear, we'd fall asleep, peaceful, safe, true. The next morning, I would help chop vegetables.

"Don't join!" Amy was joking but maybe she felt the wandering in me.

We walked to the T and hopped on the train which had just pulled up, wheezing and chugging. Amy sat and I stood the few stops, my mind racing, round and round. Krishnas, Bubbie, Dear Abby, Queen Jezebel. Her fiery eyes had dipped into me, strengthened me, gave me some odd purpose—no one understood her yet she didn't sway from herself, even though the price she paid was her life. The truth of what was happening with my family, all the secrets, threatened to bust open, spill from my guts like some broken pumpkin, the seeds going in every direction, messy. The idea of Queen Jezebel somehow glued me together, urged me to break through the murk, keep saying the truth, seeking the truth.

Bubbie's stop was next and I decided to go see her. "Amy, call me when you get to Maine."

"We have no phones up there! My parents' idea of roughing it, nearest phone is down the road at the general store. Except my Dad has a secret phone for emergencies. I'll be back in August to visit colleges and we can go together, okay?"

At the Coolidge Corner stop, we hugged goodbye and I jumped out, marveling at how organized Amy was. I hadn't even thought about college, only that I might run away to Rachel's dorm at BU in

September. Well, it was only the end of June and I had a whole senior year to think about it.

My body felt jumpy from the speed, my mouth was dry and I needed a mint. There was a *Dunkin' Donuts* right by Bubbie's apartment. Bubbie loved donuts, especially cinnamon coated, and I knew she'd appreciate a few, but I didn't feel like stopping. The sugary smells drifted as I crossed to Bubbie's building, a large clean brick six story with two gardens and thick railings for all the older people who lived there. Bubbie didn't leave her apartment much, but I probably should have called first. She lived on the fourth floor and as I walked up the steps with the heat blasting, I wondered if old people stayed colder. Chicken soup with onion smells turned my stomach. I felt claustrophobic as I knocked on Bubbie's door.

There was a rustling, shuffle of feet as she yelled, "Who's there?"

"It's Jezebel, Bubbie."

Bubbie opened the door slowly, patted my face and led me inside.

Her apartment was pre-war with two bedrooms, a small kitchen and a cozy living room, really quiet. I worried about her and all those stairs. In her living room was a long, faded light green couch that had a wilted flower pattern with an ottoman which had a striped pattern from a previous couch.

"Sit, bubelah, sit."

Bubbie's hair was long and braided down to her waist, still black scattered with silver, her face wide with a pudgy nose that had thick, square glasses perched on the bridge. Her cheeks were soft with white skin and not very many wrinkles for her seventy-nine years. Her teeth were straight, white and false because I had seen them in the glass. She had a sturdy build, was from the Ukraine, and when she spoke Yiddish it was sprinkled with English words. By Bubbie's magazines was a picture of her standing by an old car at her first apartment, Blue Hill Avenue in Dorchester. That was before I was born. Sometimes she'd tell me stories from that time, and from her past. She had been a socialist in the Ukraine at the time of the pogroms, it was dangerous, so she escaped and moved to Boston. My parents didn't talk much about their families or their history and when they did relay stories they were too short and their voices faded, off to another place with words trailing, unfinished. Like they were all sad stories. Bubbie was my only hope for family history, and when she told me stories, her face became alive and I understood most of what she said, except some of the Yiddish.

When Bubbie was living in Dorchester she was a baby nurse, and Mom told me that Bubbie cared for me in my first year, to help Mom out. That's probably why I felt close to her, and really comfortable, like a pillow.

The black and white photo was from the 40's, and Bubbie was leaning against the car, smiling. "Bubbie, do you have more pictures?"

"Eh, I'm tired, next time, I'll show you, I have." She was usually more awake and asked about school which I liked— I'd tell her everyday things about my friends, the books I was reading— she seemed happy to hear. When Mom asked she never listened to my answer and Dad, well, he barely spoke with me these days. Once Bubbie had told me Dad was a wild teenager and she beat him for discipline, she said this without shame or regret, like that's what they did back then. The beatings probably damaged him, made him, well, bad in some way. Bubbie loved me so I could never ever tell her what he did. In case she thought I was lying. In case she'd say it wasn't anything. In case she stopped loving me.

"Come back tomorrow, meyn kind, I'll have pictures. We'll talk, eat." She opened a drawer that was hidden under the table's edge and removed a white envelope. "Here, take."

"Thanks, Bubbie." It probably contained a five-dollar bill, like always. She patted my face, put her head on a pillow, closed her eyes. I wondered what it was like getting old. I counted the moles on her face and she stirred and mumbled some words in Yiddish. At that moment, I decided I didn't want to live past thirty-five. My face was warm as I watched her fall into sleep. Don't die, I yelled silently, I need you. Her head tilted against the pillow with her braid squished against the side of her face. She didn't look comfortable, and I couldn't sleep that way. Old people must be so tired.

My mouth was sand and I needed water. The speed crash had started, I hated that part, grouchy and edgy. Short, loud snores came from Bubbie's open mouth which at first mesmerized me with their pattern, honk honk, beat, honk honk. Then they annoyed me, so I got up.

In her kitchen, I stuck my head under the sink faucet and drank big, warm, rusty gulps. The cabinets held jars of weird food, and I opened them all, not really knowing what I was looking for. I wondered who took Bubbie shopping, who helped her. She was all alone in this apartment, and I didn't think my Dad visited often, unless he snuck here, like me.

Bubbie's bedroom door was open so I walked in. There was a pretty, light green silk scarf hanging on a doorknob to her closet. It smelled like her—tea and lemons. I put it around my neck.

Next to her room was the guest room. The curtains were open and light from the garden made pretty patterns on the bed. Lying on the soft, yellow blanket, with my head on the pillows, I pictured what it would be like living here. I'd have my own room, Boston and Harvard Square were close, and Bubbie would have company. Except the whole place smelled like old people, and maybe she wouldn't want me there all the time. And Mom would be so mad at me. The thought of that made me so irritated, I jumped up and left the room.

Bubbie was snoring away on the couch. "I'm going to borrow this scarf, Bubbie, I'll bring it back." Quietly, I closed the front door, walked down the staircase holding my nose, and stopped by a meter on the sidewalk.

What next? Speed crashes sucked, made me feel so bad, skin dry, everything strange. Weed mellowed the landing, and Amy had a friend Harry who always had a stash. Even though Amy didn't get high, she had good connections. But I was too tired. I wished for something, someone, that would take away the hole that was gnawing inside.

Not Eric, he was back at college and I didn't even know if he was my boyfriend anymore. Someone new and undiscovered.

I leaned against the hard, metal meter and watched cars drive by. Sunday drivers, slowly enjoying a ride. I never understood how that was enjoyable—riding in a car, not going anywhere in particular, just hearing the hum of tires, while stores, trees, scenic views whizzed by.

The sun on my face almost felt like a hug, and I closed my eyes, opening them when I sensed someone there. An old man with a ripped coat held out his battered cup and I gave him the rest of my change.

Time to head home. The T was too slow and I didn't feel like waiting. There were lots of cars on the road, so at Commonwealth I stuck out my thumb. After a minute, a dark blue Chrysler with a dented fender pulled over. An older guy was driving and he seemed normal, clean shirt, average face, like the counter waiter at Brigham's.

"Newton?" I said.

He nodded and I climbed in, making sure my door was unlocked.

His front seat was clean with an old coffee cup stuck between the seats amongst Kleenex and spearmint lifesavers. I leaned against the car window and watched apartment buildings, pedestrians, pigeons. After a few minutes, I heard something rustle and I glanced over. He had his penis out and was rubbing it as he snuck glances at my boobs, his eyes going from the road to my boobs while he touched himself. I didn't feel scared, just curious. But just in case, I held the door handle.

He saw me looking. "Will you touch it?" He sounded sad and hopeful.

I knew the feel of a penis and had no interest in touching his.

"No thanks."

We were almost in Newton, home turf. I heard more rustling and noticed he had put the penis away.

He dropped me three blocks from my house.

"Thank you," I said.

He raised his hand, slow motion, eyes heavy. He seemed pitiful and I wanted to say something profound, like, "Best not to expose yourself, find a wife instead, or another hobby..." something. He was a creep, yet seemed an accidental weirdo. I walked three blocks, late for dinner, and they didn't care and neither did I because I wasn't hungry. At home, I clunked down on my bed and watched time show itself through atoms and dust, the fading light of day making animal shadows through the curtains.

CHAPTER THREE: TREACLE TARTS

Around 8:30, Rachel came in from her dance class.

"Hey, Jez." She took off her jean jacket and lay on the bed. "I'm exhausted." She sipped from the water glass that was always on her side table.

"A guy showed me his dick."

Her eyebrows raised. "You mean that guy from the playground?"

Everyone knew about him, this tall lanky guy who told kids he had candy in his pocket and when we reached in, surprise, no candy, just his penis.

"No, not that guy. I hitched from Bubbie's, and the driver took out his penis."

Rachel reached her hand over and I held it, her nails freshly painted pink. "Jez, that's really dangerous. I'll pick you up if you're stuck somewhere, or from Bubbie's there's the T. What did you do?"

"He wasn't serious, just a perv. I should paint my nails, yours are pretty."

"You'd ruin them too fast."

"That's true." For some reason I usually had dirt under my fingernails.

"Be more careful, Jezzy, you're too reckless."

Voices came from the living room. "Who's over?"

"The college students, they're playing cards with Mom and organizing for the impeach Nixon rally next weekend at Boston Common."

"She's not painting?"

"Guess not tonight."

Mom was politically active as was my whole family, especially for anti-Vietnam war activities. When I was eleven I'd argue with kids in my class who were for the war, these ignorant kids brainwashed by their parents. Once the teacher took me to the side and said, "Politics are for adults, Jezebel, you should think of more pleasant matters." With the Vietnam war raging overseas, death counts were ridiculous, and those were the matters that were important to me, but I didn't say that. Mom brought Rachel and I to protests and she'd have these organizing meetings which always looked like cards. Dad wasn't that active, though he contributed money to political candidates and read a ton. He'd get the paper from the John Birch society which was a right-wing organization and when I asked him about it he said, "It's important to know what the enemy is doing."

Politics was one area my parents agreed on. That and classical music—they had season tickets to the Boston Symphony Orchestra and that's the music they played on our living room stereo. When I couldn't fall asleep at night Mom would put on Beethoven's Sixth Symphony and before the storm sequence I would be asleep.

A sweet smell emanated from the kitchen, thick with caramel. Mom had made treacle tarts, thin buttery crust with gooey, hot, rich treacle, open face with tons of golden syrup. I felt hopeful.

"Rach, Mom made tarts, want some?" I let go of her hand.

"I'm good."

Without them noticing I peeked at Mom's company. She was at the dining room table with four of the regular students from Boston College. Chip, who's lap Mom was sitting on, was twenty-five with medium length brown hair with bangs, preppy looking, cute, wearing a polo. With his back to me sat Alan, a big husky guy with a mustache who Mom said liked me, and across from him was Henri, the first openly gay man I ever met. Henri had long silky hair and always wore a scarf, and tonight he had on a green paisley one. A cute Latino guy was leaning into him, a new boyfriend, who wore a pink flowered scarf that didn't match his rugged looks, so I guessed Henri forced him to wear it. Everyone was holding cards, with drinks and snacks scattered on the table. The treacle tarts sat prominently in the middle, calling to me—Mom had also made a trifle, Dad's favorite, a dessert with layered custard, sponge cake, fruit cocktail, covered in whipped cream.

Usually Mom's political meetings were on Friday or Saturday, with Sunday nights quiet. Rachel and I would do our homework while Mom painted on the back porch right behind where they were playing cards. I saw the tubes of oils on the paint-stained table beside her chair, ready and waiting for her painting session.

Before I went to get some tarts, I went through the pile of mail that was on the kitchen counter. There was an envelope with my name and I tore open the seal. Inside was a laminated ID card with my name and birthdate two years older than I really was. My fake ID! Eric had helped me get it since he was already eighteen. Now I could go to clubs! Hear music! Meet people!

I felt like I was holding my ticket to freedom.

Alan came into the kitchen and I quickly stuck the ID in my jeans pocket. "Hi, Jezebel. Come join us." He tapped his cheek for a kiss, which I ignored, and we walked into the dining room.

With a drink in one hand, cards in the other, Mom barely glanced at me as she lifted her shoulder. "Jezebel doesn't want our company, Alan, she's busy with her own life. Henri, it's your turn." Waving her cards at him, she moved her head touching Chip's.

Chip shrugged as he picked up his beer bottle. Henri gave me air kisses as his boyfriend peeked at his cards. From the den, Dad's TV blasted laugh tracks from a sitcom. It felt sad looking at the trifle with Dad downstairs.

"It's Sunday, Mom. Why aren't you painting?" The words came out too loud.

Mom was the most relaxed when she painted. With her oils, she'd create these worlds far away from her real life. The painting on her easel now, which she was almost done with, was of a Native American reservation with sun-kissed adobe structures, mountains towering with light brown dirt, blended with a cloudy sky that showed pastel blue patches. The foreground showed two Native American women with long braids that framed their faces, light cotton shawls, kneeling, making clay pots that blended with dirt, somehow getting across a mood of quiet. Mom always painted women who were strong, focused, working in a simple external world with others, in an environment of nature. They were incredible paintings, hung all over our house, signed with a simple 'S' for Sylvia.

"We're organizing," Mom said, as Chip shifted her on his lap and didn't meet my eye. The whole scene annoyed me. They were playing cards, not doing political stuff. I reached for the plate of tarts. "Rachel asked me for tarts, Mom, can we have a few?" I took three of the biggest ones and balanced them in my hands, as Mom, for a brief second, focused on me.

"Did you have dinner? There's some cold cuts in the fridge, you can take them in your room." In other words, go away.

Alan pulled out the chair next to him. "Jezebel, have a seat, you can be my partner."

"Oh shush, Alan." Mom waved her cards at him. "There's no partners and she has better things to do." She turned away from me, done. "Henri, it's your turn, we don't have all night."

Alan reached for my arm and I pulled away before he could touch me. I kicked his fat leg, hard. A shocked look flashed on his face, but then he smiled and I stuck out my tongue, holding the tarts close. He must have been thirty-years old. Dirty old man. I didn't even want to join their card game, with Mom acting like Chip was her boyfriend and Dad alone downstairs.

I went into our bedroom and closed the door.

The tarts were warm, with a crisp, flakey crust, gooey and delicious.

"Dad should play cards with everyone," I said.

On her bed in pink baby-doll pajamas, Rachel stretched her leg straight in the air with her hands on each side. She switched her legs back and forth, back and forth. "He has his own poker night with his guy friends."

"Dad seems depressed, don't you think? He never talks to me."

"He's not depressed, he's distracted with work and business worries."

"Does he talk with you?"

Rachel sighed. "Sometimes, Jez."

"It's always so tense."

"I guess."

Agree with me, Rachel, see what I see. Talk about how fucked-up this all is. Mom on Chip's lap, Dad ignoring, and the other stuff I told her that she didn't believe, that Mom had denied.

"Okay if I put on the radio?" I loved WBCN in Boston and hoped Little Bill was on.

"Sure."

Bill and I were friends in middle school until he went to Newton North for high school and I went to Newton South. He was almost famous, really cute, and knew everything about the music scene. I had the thought to call him. He'd remember me since I starred in *Amahl and the Night Visitors* in ninth grade. We could reconnect and go clubbing. He'd be taken by me, we'd fall in love, and he'd introduce me to all the famous musicians. I would find the best jazz piano teacher in the whole world.

"While you're at the dance internship I'm going to study jazz piano," I said.

Rachel picked up a book and got under her covers. "That's a great idea, Jez." Her long hair splayed on the white pillow case and I had the urge to braid it like we did when we were kids.

Also, I wanted to beg her, please please Rachel come to the beach house with us.

I climbed into my bed and grabbed one of my comfort books, *Pippi Longstocking*, which I had from grade school—getting the scholastic book club list was my favorite part of school. Mom let me order up to five books and I would read them over and over. The tart crust was buttery on my lips, the treacle sweet on my tongue. Pippi was drinking coffee on her porch attached to her house that she owned without any parents, just a monkey and a horse. She looked really happy with her pigtails straight out, freckles bold on her face, all safe and free with her animals.

CHAPTER FOUR: HARMONICA MAN

Friday when I was packing for our move to the beach house Amy called to go dancing. "You can sleep over," she said.

"Excellent! My fake ID came and I can get us both in." Or so I hoped.

At seven I hopped on my boy's bike named Strider and rode down Center Street. My skirt kept hitching up to my waist so I was basically riding in my underwear. I kept pulling it down but my bike wobbled every time I jerked my skirt. The halter top I wore showed my stomach, but I had knee-high Frye boots and a jean jacket covering my bare back so I thought it was a good outfit for wherever we ended up.

I buzzed past Brigham's, the deli, the dry-cleaner, and down Beacon Street to Amy's where I rolled my bike into her back yard. Her parents were strict and I didn't think they liked me so I knocked on her back door lightly.

She answered right away, as if she had been waiting for me. I thought her outfit was awful for clubbing: a blue wrap-around skirt to her knee and a pretty, flowered blouse. But I didn't say anything because she had a big smile when she saw me.

"Wait here, I'll grab the keys." There was a television in the background and I heard Amy say goodbye to her parents. They were a nice, boring, rich couple who I barely saw.

"Where are we going?" I said as Amy started her mother's Cadillac.

"There's this club on Commonwealth Ave. that has great dance music. It starts at seven-thirty, you don't need an ID, at least that's what I heard but if we do, you have yours, right?"

"Yes! It just came in the mail." I touched my back pocket to make sure it was there. It was early evening and we drove about ten minutes when Amy said, "That's the club. Let's park." It was on the corner and we got a parking space at the next block. Amy was a careful driver and she could parallel park really well.

When we got out of the car I turned my back to Amy. "Is my skirt up my butt?"

She laughed and smoothed my skirt down. We walked past brick apartment buildings to the club, which was lit outside with neon signs and a disco ball that left colors on the sidewalk.

"I hope we get in," Amy said, nodding at the people lined up. Her lips were shiny and thicker than usual.

"I like your lips," I said, puckering mine. She handed me the tube and I put some on. When we got to the bouncer, I smiled and walked past him and then felt a hand on my shoulder.

"ID."

As I gave him my fake ID Amy grabbed my arm to show we were together.

"I need a driver's license," the bouncer said, and handed me back my card. "These cards are bogus. And I'd say you're about fifteen. Next!"

The next group pushed past us.

"Sixteen," I said, but he didn't hear me.

We walked away and stopped by a big, green mailbox on the sidewalk. I examined my card which looked legitimate with my picture and my real birth date two years older, making me eighteen, Massachusetts drinking age.

"Shoot, I can't believe he didn't take it," I said. "I'm almost seventeen and I think I look older, well, sometimes at least."

We decided to try another club on Mass Ave. in Cambridge.

"There's a new blues woman playing at Jack's and I read in the Phoenix it's great dance music," Amy said.

Back in her Mom's caddy, we sang along with Bob Dylan on the radio. *Lay lady lay, lay across my big brass bed...* Boston was summertime hopping and we drove past people hanging on their stoops with music blasting from boom boxes. On a busy corner a group of women faced the street and held signs that said, "Our right to decide" and "Impeach Nixon!" Cars honked as they drove past and Amy held her horn long and loud.

"Our right to decide about the president?" I couldn't keep up with all the political stuff that was going on these days.

"Abortion rights," Amy said.

I nodded. "Oh yeah, that's really important."

We parked and walked a few blocks to the club on Massachusetts Avenue. Surprisingly, there was no line, and Amy and I snuck through the door unnoticed and stood inside by a long bar crowded with people. The bartenders wore striped rugby shirts and there were bowls of pretzels and peanuts on the bar, with the lights low. Smoked-filled air moved above us.

"We did it, we got in," I said, squished against a pole. "I think we were supposed to pay cover."

Amy shrugged. "No one was at the door so I think we're good."

"Get me a beer if you can, I'm going to pee."

In the bathroom, I reached for the chain on my neck that had a silver coke spoon on it. The vial in my skirt pocket was given to me by Eric the last time we were together. He was the only one I knew rich enough to buy cocaine, and he was only rich because he sold weed. He said this coke was pure so only take a little. I put a small amount on the spoon and sniffed hard, then did the same in the other nostril. Instantly I felt like this was my night, like I owned it. Of course I would find a piano teacher. Of course someone would fall in love with me.

There was a lady at the sink with pale white skin, white hair in a bun, putting on bright red lipstick, and I watched, mesmerized at how she lined her lips with pencil and then, dab dab dab, expertly applied the lipstick.

"Do you want some, honey?" Her eyes were kind as she turned my way. "You have such a pretty face; some make-up would look nice on you." She smiled and I wanted to say, "Mom!" and let her make up my face. Instead I just shook my head and left, glancing at her high heels. My mom wore high heels and dresses and knew how to apply stuff like that lady, and I wondered why she never taught me, even though I didn't want to wear make-up. Just, it would have been nice to know how.

People were crowding in and the dance floor was filled with bodies. Amy grabbed me and yelled, "Let's dance, Jez, bar was too crowded, we can get drinks later."

We weaved our way to the front. An old Black man, wide-brimmed hat, lots of teeth, played guitar. Watching him closely I saw he had six fingers.

"Amy, he has six fingers," I screamed. And boy, could he play. The drummer, a guy wearing sun glasses and a cowboy hat with a beard and mustache, kept a light beat, and there was a really cute harmonica player with wavy brown hair to his shoulders, wailing on his harp. There was something familiar about him and I thought he might be the harmonica player in the alley, the one I saw just last week on that awful family dinner night. The one who held out his hand and offered me escape. Dancing in front of him I caught his eye and he nodded at me or maybe it was just his movement, but I kept him in my sight.

A woman with long, thick, red hair entered from the wings, sat at the piano and everything else seemed to fade in the background. As chords splayed from her fingers, she sang about a mighty tight woman, her voice piercing inside me. She sang my desires, things I couldn't put into words. The harmonica wailed in a sexy cry. We danced, swayed, disappeared in the music, the notes coursed through every space inside me. I was the piano player, right up there on stage, under the spotlight.

After their set, which was way too short, the piano player lady got a beer and moved to the back of the room. Something in me thought that she could teach me piano, teach me to play like her. It wasn't so far-fetched; I already knew how to play basics. The atmosphere, being in the club, dancing, gave me confidence, and I walked over where she was sitting on an old piano at the back of the club, her band standing around her. Everyone was talking and laughing as I wormed my way through, standing in front of her.

"Hey, darling!" she said, her long red hair falling over her face.

It was so loud in the club I had to yell. "Hi! I love your music! Can you teach me jazz piano?"

There was a split second of silence where the clatter of glasses and the pouring of drinks seemed to freeze midair. Then it erupted into noise. The drummer burst into laughter and the piano player threw her head back laughing and the harmonica player's eyes smiled at me as he moved close. "Hmmm," he said in a mellow smooth voice. "She plays the blues pretty girl yeah gotta know the difference between jazzy jazz jazz and blues." All the while he nodded his head and looked at me with soft, green eyes. His body was lanky with loose movements and I just knew he was the man I saw in the alley, but at that point I wanted to disappear.

They all started talking about something else, someone new came over and I took a step back, then another, as heat blasted up my head.

Blues lady called out to me. "Darling, look for someone named Sparky. Jazz, blues, they have it all."

Sparky! I got a name! But first I had to learn the difference between blues and jazz.

Back at the bar, Amy had ordered two beers and I gulped mine down in five swallows.

"I just embarrassed myself, I'm such a jerk," I said, watching her take small sips. "How do you sip beer? It's meant to be chugged," I yelled over loudness.

"I don't like it," she said, pushing her hair behind her ears. When I turned, the harmonica player was beside me, his green eyes smiling like trees in springtime.

"Hey, jazzy girl." His lips were soft and his voice, a rhythm.

"Oh, hi!"

He smiled a slow grin, a sleepy invitation. "What's your name?" He was wearing a black tee shirt and loose black pants, his arms were thin but muscular and a tattoo peeked from the edge of his left sleeve. Someone pushed me and my body bumped into him. He put his arm around me and left it there as warmth spread through me.

"Jezebel."

His voice was in my ear. "Jezebel."

Holding my gaze, he traced his finger on my arm. "You play piano?"

Nodding, I would have said yes to anything, he was so gorgeous.

"Come jam with us, afternoons at Berklee. We'll help you find a teacher. Or Sparky might show up." He moved closer, smelled of spice, his hair brushed my face, and then he was gone, back onstage for the next set.

Amy was beside me. "Wow, cute!"

Words were caught in my throat and I mumbled, "I know. I'm in love with him."

"He likes you." Amy nudged me with her body.

It was *the* harmonica man. I couldn't lose him again! The guy in the alley. And now I had a teacher to search for. Sparky. Afternoons at Berklee School of Music. I would definitely find my way there.

The second set started, the music was loud and we pulled each other back on the dance floor. Guys bought us drinks, Amy said no but I drank, danced, poured sweat, drank more, merged into a sound dream, lost in music, freed. Dance trance. Time was irrelevant, the club so crowded and loud, the harmonica wailed, the beat of percussion, the pulse of my own body.

And then, I lost track.

My eyes popped open. It was morning. The sound of waves crashed against a beach, an open window blew warm air and I was in a strange bed. Where was I?

How did I get here and who was this man beside me? I hoped it was the harmonica man and when I glanced over I saw a pale face, short hair, scruffy beard. Who was this guy? Last night. I had a vague recollection of Amy wanting to leave, me saying no, thinking I'd wait for the harmonica man, feeling free and fearless. Memory of a drive, rolled around in bed, had some sort of sex? This surf outside, this beach, was it Rockport? Gloucester? Where did I tell Mom I slept? My head was foggy from too much drink. I didn't handle alcohol well, hated this feeling, forgetting what I did, and now, the result. A strange man, a strange bed.

Must get home.

"Where's my car, I have to leave."

The man sat up with an amused expression on his face as he handed me a glass of water. He was old, late twenties at least. "You told your friend Amy to leave, said you'd find your way home, so she left. She was reluctant, but you insisted."

Okay, I messed up big time. Was Amy mad at me, did I lie to her?

She was protective of me, probably didn't want to leave me. Alcohol sucked, made me polluted, stupid.

On the drive back to Newton in his VW bug, he told me he was twenty-nine and owned a restaurant. Had I told him I was sixteen? I was relieved he wasn't a creep and didn't ditch me by the side of the road or worse, hurt me. I pulled my jean jacket around me, felt cold, my stomach queasy and mouth sour. On the radio, a Sunday morning prayer service spoke about Jesus.

Jesus, pray for me.

When we got to Newton I made him drop me at the corner of my street in case Mom looked out the window. As I went to leave he took a book from his glove compartment, wrote on the first page, and handed it to me. I stuck the book under my arm without looking at it.

"Thanks for driving me home."

There was a buzz in my head turning into an ache and the sunlight hurt my eyes. Across the street from my house on the curb a fat, orange cat sniffed at something dead, or food, it was hard to see. Batting with its paw, then sniffing, then batting—a leaf, mouse, bird? I was mesmerized until the cat glared at me. I ran up my driveway.

Dad was watching sports and I tried to bypass him but he called me over and sniffed.

"You've been smoking?" His eyes didn't leave the screen though his tone was harsh.

"My friends smoke, Dad, cigarettes are gross, they make everything smell. Where's Mom?" Change the topic, get upstairs, keep moving.

"She's at Sheila's for scrabble."

Extremely hungover, mind scrambled, I didn't want trouble so I raced up stairs. Mom was at Sheila's, an anti-war friend. Scrabble board, letter tiles, triple points. In the kitchen, I drank three glasses of water and grabbed a sleeve of shortbread cookies to bring to my room.

As I lay on my bed, I opened the book the guy had given me. It was *The Little Prince* by Antoine de Saint-Exupery, translated to English. Inside he had written, "To a truly beautiful flower," Love, Pat.

How did he know I was a beautiful flower? I didn't feel like a beautiful flower. I hadn't even remembered his name before I saw his signature. I glanced at the picture on the front cover of the thin book, of a boy with short blond hair, who was standing on, well, the edge of the earth? Looking at the sun, stars and moon. He seemed sad. I turned away and then looked back. His expression changed and he looked curious. I did this several times and each time his expression changed.

On the first page the author had dedicated this book to his friend when he was a child. One of the reasons he dedicated this to his friend was, he wrote, because he 'lives in France where he is hungry and cold.'

I lay in bed thinking about this over and over. Why was he cold? Did he live on the street? And why was he hungry? The copyright was 1943. Was France occupied then? Were the Nazis there? Was he, his friend, in a concentration camp?

Mom had been in Europe at that time. She had bomb scares, shelters, drills. Is that why she was so nervous all the time? Was she like the author's friend—hungry and cold? Mom had said her family heated their house with coal, her Mom baked tasty pies and tarts, her Dad was a charmer and gambler. He visited America once. I had a vague picture of a man wearing a well-pressed shirt buttoned to his collar, shoes that shined, with a cigarette that dangled from his mouth.

I closed the book and soon my eyes, and pictured behind my lids was the boy from the cover. He seemed barren, like the author's friend, which made me sad. I knew this was the only page I'd ever read, even though I was curious what happened to the Little Prince.

CHAPTER FIVE: FOG HORN

That Sunday, Mom and I moved to our beach house. Hull Massachusetts, on the South Shore of Boston. When Mom was twenty-two and visiting from England, my parents met there, and soon got married. Every summer since they had rented a house until five years ago when Dad bought a house on Adams Street, one block from the beach. Our house had one floor and a basement, front and back porches, a yard, three bedrooms, living room, kitchen, and a bike shed where my second bike Aragorn was kept.

Here at the beach Mom acted differently, with an air of hope and carelessness—just add sun, ocean air, cards and cocktails. Past summers when Rachel and Dad were here we had a routine of beach, a charcoal barbecue with flames blasting from lighter fluid, huge bowls of barbecue potato chips, a mixed drink for Mom and cream soda for us. Burgers. Hot dogs. Occasional steak. Ketchup. iceberg lettuce salad, toasted marshmallows perfectly browned or burnt, exploding into flames. Usually Dad only came for weekends and one week in July. Mom loved this arrangement.

While Mom drove, I wondered about this summer and what was going to happen. Rachel would be at her dance internship and preparing for college, and Dad had said he would be working more. Ever since the night at the club, the awful night when I ended up in that guy's place and couldn't remember anything, all I could think of was finding the piano teacher Sparky. And how I could find the gorgeous harmonica man again. I knew both of them were in Boston and the harmonica man had invited me to Berklee. Thankfully, I had remembered that part of the night. Boston was only an hour from our beach house but I didn't have my own car. I could borrow Mom's when she was in a good mood. I'd figure it out, somehow. I had to!

We had a small truck deliver our stuff and Mom and I arrived around noon. The house smelled like mildew, so I opened all the windows. Mine and Rachel's room had two beds, two wooden dressers, a straight back chair and a plain black side table with a Winnie-the-Pooh lamp, from childhood. Mom said she'd buy a new one except I liked Winnie-the-Pooh and all his friends.

I unpacked my three new bikinis, shorts, halter tops, flip flops, sweatshirts, three sun dressers, and my books: *The Prophet*, *On the Road*, *Siddhartha*, the two books from George's Folly about meditation and LSD. Then my comfort books: *Pippi Longstocking*, *A Wrinkle in Time*, *Harriet the Spy*, *The Long Secret*, *Honestly Katie John*, *The Hobbit*. After we unpacked I went in search of my summer friends. My trusty bike Aragorn was there in the shed and I brushed off the dust, checked the tires which needed some air, and hopped on.

The beach part was called Nantasket Beach and it was pretty flat for bike riding. My friend Carla lived three houses down. She was a year older like my sister and had just graduated from a high school in Chelsea. She was popular and seemed knowledgeable about the world in a way that I was awed by, like when she talked about the kids at her school, who dated who, what girl was wild and going down the wrong road. When she talked about that she had looked at me with a concerned expression, like I was that wild girl. But I still loved hanging with her and I loved when she expertly applied eye make-up, which I had no idea how to do.

My kickstand was stuck but at the second try it worked, and after I parked my bike, I knocked on her front door. Her mom yelled hello from some back room and I spoke through the screen door.

"It's Jezebel! Is Carla there? What? Oh, yes, thanks, good winter, you? Okay yes thanks parents good yeah we just got down today, okay, Carla home? Oh, okay, working at the cheese shop, North End, the whole summer? Oh, okay, she'll visit when she can, okay, sure I'll tell Mom hello."

Two streets over by the bay was Kate's house. Kate was really funny and nice to me, even when Carla teased that I was boy crazy. Kate gave me life tips, advised me to study hard, be a good person, don't sneak out at night.

After I knocked, her mom appeared and let me know that Kate was working all summer at a bookstore in Ann Arbor, Michigan, and that I should tell my Mom she was available for scrabble.

The gas station was at the corner of Nantasket Ave. and A street. It was humid and foggy, both warm and cool, and as I filled my tires, a family walked towards the beach, pulling a wagon with their chairs, towels and boogie boards. The kids were young. Where were all the teenagers, the ones I knew from past summers? There was a faint smell of grease that emanated from a small pizza place next to the laundromat. Kids on bikes wheeled around, and there was no one I recognized.

Last summer everyone had been down. Girls from all over. Carla from Chelsea, Kate from Brookline, Donna with the Doberman from Chelmsford, and a lot of townie boys, two that I had a crush on. Boys who lived here all year intrigued me. They were working class and tough, with their tattoos, muscles, short haircuts, walking in the middle of the street and roaring, eyes sharp as knives, looking for a challenge.

Hull was a tough town during the winter. Summer was different and the all-year-round guys sometimes went for us summer girls, and we always wanted their attention. At least I did. Last summer Jimmy was around so after I filled my tires I rode by his house. It was all closed up, windows nailed with boards. A neighbor was watering his lawn and yelled, "They moved to Revere."

I nodded and rode off. Jimmy and Revere made sense, he was always the leader of his gang and his body was the hardest with muscles even when he was ten, which is when I met him. Revere had its own beach and always held this captivating image for me. Their streets were tough and all the families were Irish Catholic. I scored my first weed there which I discovered later was oregano. I had taken three different trolleys from my house in Newton, then met a girl and bought this tiny brown package for five dollars. Her house was two-family with peeled paint, a younger sibling peeking out from behind a faded white curtain.

The girl had looked me up and down as she took my money and delivered a brown envelope, which seemed suspiciously small. I walked back to the train, past similar houses that stood wind-torn and ragged. Even the bay across the street was ominous, dark with white caps.

Revere families seemed stronger, better than mine. Their parents yelled and the kids knew they cared since they were strict in the very best way. "You're not leaving this house until you clean up the kitchen." "Get back here and do your homework." "You're coming to church, move!" Their moms were tough so they became good citizens, and even though the dads drank hard, stayed late at the bar and got into fights, and their moms smoked too many cigarettes, I had imagined their kids felt loved and secure, confident. They walked tall and had backup.

That feeling had stayed with me, somewhere deep. The question pulsed inside of me. Could you hold up your head and say that someone owned you?

I wanted that feeling. That bond. To be one of the girls who read each other's letters from school friends, gossip about who dated who, get that sense of connection. Laugh as if I knew what they meant. And, when there was a pause, when we weren't boogie boarding or spreading baby oil on our skin, lighting fireworks or making bonfires, when it was all stopped, for me there was always an empty feeling. In the summer's past, everyone seemed okay when things ended and it was time to go home. I had felt as if pieces of me were scattered and I wanted to say, 'wait, help, I just need to put these parts together.' And now, none of my gang was here, and I didn't know what I would do.

At the beach by the dunes, I leaned my bike against a sign "No Dogs Allowed: June 1 – September 15". Walking over the dunes, the sight of the ocean made my breath catch. That hadn't changed. Every year, the first time I saw the ocean made me so happy. Unlike friends, the ocean was always there.

Sitting in the cool, soft sand, my body relaxed. Waves rolled towards me, it was high tide and the fog horn sang. I counted, hoot 1, 2, 3, 4, 5, 6, 7, 8, hoot 1, 2, 3, 4, 5, 6, 7, 8, hoot.

Seagulls cried. The dark green ocean embraced me. Hello summertime.

CHAPTER SIX: CARDS AND DRINKS

The next day Mom was on the beach with her summer friends and they started their routine of drinks and cards. Later in the afternoon when I was home from a swim a man named Barry who Mom said was her 'new friend' drove up in a white Mercedes. I was sitting on the front stoop and Mom skipped out to his car wearing a pretty flowered sundress and white heels.

"Where are you going, Mom? I thought we were having a barbecue."

She shrugged one shoulder. "We can another time, I'm going to play cards. Come meet my new friend, Barry."

"Another time," I said and stared into the car. Barry was already tan with leathery skin and very white teeth which glowed as Mom approached. As they rode off he waved. Three kids raced their bikes across the sidewalk, and a neighbor I didn't recognize with a yappy dog walked past and said hello. The smell of hamburgers from other family's barbecues made my stomach growl. Unsure of my next step, I wished my sister was here.

I dialed Rachel's dorm room at Jacob's Pillow dance company where she was an intern.

"Hello?"

"Rachel! It's Jez."

"Hi! Look I just have a sec, we're on a break and I had to get another shirt, you okay?"

"No one's here and Mom...I don't know, I miss you."

"Our summer gang will be down, hang tight, Jez, it's only been a day or two." I heard talking in the background. "Get a tan for me, I'm pale from being inside all day!"

She hung up too fast and there wasn't time to explain that our gang was busy doing other stuff and Mom had already found a new guy to hang with. Rachel and I seemed to live in two different realities within our family. She wasn't affected by Mom's mood swings, their fights, Dad's weirdness. She said I was oversensitive. Maybe I was but I knew when things weren't right.

Dad came a few days later, July 4, with plans to stay the weekend. That night my parents went to Kate's parent's house for a barbecue and cards which I was invited to and said no. Eric was coming to watch fireworks and hopefully some other friends would show up. He arrived at seven with a six pack of Michelob and some weed, and before we drank, smoked or anything we had sex under my sheets, a kind of frantic, intense, desperate sex. Afterward I lit a cigarette. I was tense knowing Dad was nearby, he had a short attention span for parties and might be home any minute.

"Let's take our beers on the beach and watch the fireworks," I said, passing the cigarette to Eric.

"I'm taking a class this summer." He blew a smoke ring.

"Yeah, you said."

He took a long drag. "We're going out with other people, right?"

No one had spoken that aloud yet. My face heated up and I grabbed the cigarette, glancing sideways. He was looking at me expectantly. What was I supposed to say? No, please be with only me? That's what I felt. I knew I had no right, though, because I knew I wouldn't be with only him, especially if he was gone all summer.

"Sure," I said, stamping out the cigarette in a clam shell by my bed. We were doomed in any case because Eric was possessive when he saw guys check me out. Still, him saying that out loud first sucked.

On the beach bonfires were blazing, there were loud bangs of firecrackers exploding. Soon the real fireworks started. The colors and patterns were magnificent and the show was way too short with the finale a red, white and blue flag that sparkled. I wondered if my parents were watching from their party. Mom said she hated this holiday, being British, but she really liked fireworks.

Eric left at midnight even though I begged him to stay on the couch in the living room so we could hang out the next day. All the crowds of people celebrating had made me feel lonesome.

"Got to get back," he said.

I kissed him and sat on the stoop as he drove away. Fuck you to all my friends who weren't here, and fuck you to Eric. I took a sip of the beer that was warm now and touched the pile of sand on the step with my bare foot, making a pattern. Amidst bangs and booms, Sulphur smells, sparklers, parents carrying tired children, I stood, went inside and climbed under my covers. My parents weren't home yet which was unusual—Dad was an early bird.

Their yells woke me not much later.

Dad's voice was first, loud, the fight must have started on their way home. Didn't they care that I was asleep? "...all I do is work to provide for this family." Then Mom's voice from the kitchen, her too-many-drinks voice, squeaky, slurred. "You're a bore. I don't know why you bother going, you hate parties." Then Dad, his voice level raised so loud I covered my ears. "Want a little peace, not this aggravation..." Then Mom's fake laugh, the one that mocked as the guest room door slammed and Mom's door closed.

Nobody cared that I was here. I was drowning, grabbed by an undertow. Dear sorcerer of the sea, take me far away, please, help me.

Errant firecrackers, distant echoes. Finally, silence. I drifted.

Dad left early the next day before I got up, his overnight bag gone from the hall closet. Mom slept late and I didn't want to be around when she woke with her hangover. I gathered my beach stuff.

Cool sand greeted me and at the edge of the water there was a pool of minnows, shimmering. They swam together and then disappeared underneath the crevices of mud. They reappeared, peeking their tiny heads. I was hypnotized with their routine. Mist came off the ocean and the waves were gentle as the tide flowed.

Small shells and stones were abundant when the tide ebbed and I picked up stones, skimmed them over the water and watched them skip once, twice, three times and one of them five times. For years I had collected sea glass. The pieces were stored in a glass jar next to my bed. Each year sea glass was more elusive and a find was special—especially blue which seemed almost extinct.

Frustration filled me. The summer had just started and already things were weird. The ocean sounds and smells helped me calm down but I knew I couldn't live here on the sand, that I had to see my parents again at some point. Mom was so happy before Dad came, why wasn't she happy when he was around?

When I was hungry I walked back and Mom was making tea.

I opened the refrigerator door. "Why did Dad leave?"

She turned. "Good morning, darling, want some tea?" Her face was drawn, tired, her eyes red.

"Mom, why?"

Her mouth tightened. "He had work."

In the fridge was a Sara Lee coffee cake, family size, and I grabbed it. Mom had a Teflon pan and was heating butter—when she first bought Teflon she was so excited at its newness and how she didn't need butter, but ended up using butter anyway since she loved it. "Want some eggs?" I shook my head and cut a large piece of coffee cake. Thirty seconds in the toaster oven would do the trick.

"Don't eat that whole thing, Jezebel."

"I'm hungry," I said, as I waited for the ding. Then I brought the whole thing to the kitchen table and sat. "It's Dad's summer vacation too," I said, tearing off a large chunk. Not that I wanted him here, I just felt bad. He paid for this house and we were his family.

"He had a golf game." She put milk and sugar in her tea.

"I heard your fight." The icing had started to melt over the cinnamon, warm and gooey, just the way I liked it.

"Oh, that. Just…nothing, he doesn't like the beach." She stood with her tea watching a dog on a long leash pee on our lawn. The day was warm, sunny, a perfect beach day.

"Yes, he does like the beach. You chased him away."

She turned towards me, her tea cup wobbly. "Are you taking his side?"

Cinnamon butter mixed with icing, delicious. I kept biting until half was finished.

"No, Mom, I don't have a side."

That week Mom spent most of her time with Barry—cards, drinks, more cards, more drinks— and I did what was familiar and lost myself in the sand, ocean, mist, waves, the stillness of moonlight. I searched for answers in my books, seeing if meditation would help me, reading about Dr. Leary's LSD trips. And mostly, I planned how to find Sparky. I'd need to get to Boston, ask around in the clubs. Find harmonica man. Join his band and be whisked away on a road tour.

CHAPTER SEVEN: QUINN

Mom had a hair appointment for Tuesday, July 15, on Newbury Street. Usually once she was at the beach she never left, so I guessed she wanted to look pretty for leather-faced Barry. She asked me if I wanted to go and I jumped at a chance to explore Berklee College of Music, see if I could find harmonica man and maybe even the teacher Sparky.

Mom drove. There were a lot of rotaries going to Boston and at the first one Mom didn't yield, she just stopped, and a car behind us honked which made her so nervous she pumped the gas and jerked our car around with the guy's horn blasting. I turned around and gave him the middle finger which he didn't see. I felt so bad for Mom who lit one of her five cigarettes a day.

I flipped on the radio.

"This is Fats and you're listening to WBCN, and we're in Boston. We're honoring Duke Ellington who is playing with his orchestra at Jazz Workshop." A song started and I listened closely to the piano, pretending to play along, hoping knowledge would miraculously creep into my fingers.

Another rotary loomed ahead and Mom gripped the steering wheel holding her breath. There were no cars behind us but she stopped.

"Just yield, Mom."

She turned her head, back and forth, waiting for any cars that might appear.

"Go, Mom."

She jerked the car around and soon we were on another straight away.

"I should have stayed at the beach," she said, her voice sharp and tight.

"I can drive."

She didn't answer, just switched off the radio and held her breath.

"I'm headed to Berklee Music School today, Mom. I'm going to see about taking piano lessons."

Mom stamped her cigarette in the metal ashtray. "I should take lessons again, I enjoyed them so much." She pulled off the highway into a garage and I felt annoyed, my stomach clenched. I wish she'd just be happy for me and encourage me to pursue this. I hated myself for telling her anything and expecting she'd be happy.

Her hair salon was on Newbury Street and I wanted to make sure she knew her way, that she didn't get lost or fall down nervous on the street. She seemed so vulnerable with her high heels, nice dress, kerchief wrapped like Elizabeth Taylor. People said Mom resembled her, with the same black hair and blue eyes, cute little nose.

After a few blocks we hugged goodbye, with plans for our rendezvous later.

At Boston Common, I heard bells of the Hare Krishnas from a corner by the benches, and considered stopping there. I'd find the cute Krishna guy and take his book, we'd talk about spiritual ideas and he'd give me advice. Maybe he was from a fucked-up family too and that's why he joined the Krishnas. But harmonica man and Sparky were my focus, so instead I crossed the street, walked a few blocks until I found a building with a small sign, "Berklee College of Music."

Sounds of instruments came from upstairs windows. I heard piano, horns, a cymbal. Following the music, I ran up the stairs to the third floor. Most of the noise was coming from the end of the hall where I found a huge rehearsal studio with a lot of people milling around. I stepped through the door and saw there was a stage set-up with a white baby grand piano, an electronic keyboard next to the piano, a few saxophones on their stands, a drum set and conga drums, and various guitars. Musicians were warming up, doing scales, talking, and immediately my eyes glued on the piano player who was a tall Black man with a mustache and goatee. I wondered if that was Sparky. Could I go ask? After embarrassing myself at Jack's I thought I'd better wait, check out the scene first.

There was another guy who was faced away, with long, wavy brown hair. When he turned around he looked my way and his soft green eyes pierced mine—it was him—the harmonica man from Jack's! He smiled and waved when he saw me and I almost started jumping up and down, I was so happy.

"Wow, look who's here, it's the bar girl." He walked towards me, his movements smooth and rhythmic, his head with a slight bounce. "Are you here to jam with us?" He took my hand.

Heat flushed my cheeks, having misrepresented the extent of my piano talents. "Is it okay if I just listen? I'm really not good enough, that's why I wanted a teacher, you know, I need some lessons." I forced my mouth closed, feeling like I was babbling.

He laughed. "No worries, we're rehearsing for our tour, come listen. Jezebel, right?"

"Yes." He remembered my name he remembered my name he loves me.

The harmonica man got me a metal chair and placed it near the stage, grabbing sheet music off a stand. "Here, follow along if you can."

There were people coming in standing by the windows and more musicians took the stage. "Is it okay that I'm here?"

"Of course."

The tech guy came over holding wires. "Help me with the mics, would ya?" He glanced at me and I felt out of place. The outfit I had on felt silly, a tight red tee that said 'Vineyard Sweets' with a picture of an ice-cream cone.

"This is Jezebel, she's a piano player," the harmonica man said. The tech guy nodded and walked away. "Yeah, just hang out, we can talk after our set." Harmonica man ran his finger down my arm and smiled. As he turned to go onstage, I realized I didn't know his name.

"Hey, what's your name?" He moved his face close to mine and his breath smelled like cinnamon, his lips smooth and yummy looking. "Quinn."

Quinn and Jezebel. The thought made me blush.

More people entered and stood around and there was a guy by the door who directed people and turned away curious students. When a clean-shaven man who wore a pressed grey suit and carried a suitcase entered, everyone got ready. He stood beside me and looked down. "Who are you?" His eyes weren't kind and his mouth had a sour expression.

Quinn sauntered over. "It's groovy, Steve, she's with me, she's a piano player."

Steve flicked his hand toward the windows and Quinn walked me over as I clutched my sheet music. Steve sat in my chair and took papers from his briefcase as Quinn squeezed my hand and whispered, "He's uptight, don't worry," and walked back to the stage.

Saxophones drums percussion harmonica guitars bass piano. The songs began. We nodded our heads, tapped our feet, moved, breathed with the sound.

Each song they played made me experience a new emotion. I felt like yelling them out. Sad! Bliss! Heaven! But of course I didn't, I just swayed with the music and watched Quinn who kept smiling at me, when it wasn't his turn to play.

Thirty minutes later they finished, energy high as musicians bantered with one another and unplugged from amps. The suit guy spoke with the musicians and all the other observers were either greeting musicians or leaving. No one said anything to me and I felt awkward and didn't know if I should leave. I pretended to study the sheet music which was pretty complicated, while sneaking glances at Quinn, who was speaking with the pretty lead singer. The thought that she was probably his girlfriend made me panicky, so I started toward the door.

"Hey, Jezebel, wait up." He kissed the woman on her cheek and came over, took my hand and stood real close. "Did you like the music?"

"It was great, really smooth."

He faced me and titled his head. "Tour starts tomorrow, New Haven. Come along?"

The dream of touring with a band, with a gorgeous guy, learning music, playing piano, flashed before me. This was my chance for escape! Except it was impossible, unless I really ran away. "I don't think I can."

He nodded and his face was close to mine. "Want to come over, we can hang out for a bit. Jezebel." The way he whispered my name gave me chills and I said yes. While he said his goodbyes, there was a surreal moment where I floated above everything and felt a mystifying kind of hopefulness.

As we walked out of the building he took my hand and I wished I didn't have to meet Mom, wished I could stay with him, go to New Haven, be on tour. Change my direction. It was kind of miraculous sitting on the beach just last week, wishing for a music scene and here I was in it.

We walked past buildings, stores, restaurants and I barely noticed anything, just the warmth of his hand, his body close. "Hey Quinn, do you know a piano player named Sparky? The lead singer of your band told me to find him, that he'd teach me jazz piano."

Quinn shook his head. "I can ask around, sweet girl."

We entered a large brick building and walked up two flights. Quinn unlocked a door into a big open space. Long windows faced the street with sun shining through, making everything light, with a big ceiling fan that cooled the space. A rocking chair, small couch and a mattress covered by a purple Indian bedspread were in the main room, with a kitchen by the front door where a tall, lean Black man with dreadlocks stood at the sink washing dishes. Blues played on a nearby radio. There was the smell of bread and coffee.

"Brother Lawrence, meet Jezebel."

Lawrence turned off the water, wiped his hands and bowed. "Me lady." I smiled and had an impulse to bow back which I didn't. "How was your gig, Quinn?"

"Perfection, we split tomorrow, even got cash from the suit."

Quinn took a cigar box from a table and motioned me over. We sat on the mattress while he rolled a joint.

Lawrence nodded. "Excellent news."

"Come have a smoke, my brother."

"Nah I got that thing, you know, across town."

"Okay, later."

Lawrence turned and bowed again. "Until next time, me lady."

After he left I said, "He's funny."

"He's the best of the best."

We sat and smoked the weed which was strong and good. Quinn got us cold glasses of pink lemonade, tart and delightful. His green eyes were hypnotic and I fell in love, right there. We kissed softly, then deeper and longer and he took off my tee and bra and I was there almost naked. He kissed my shoulders and breasts and said, "You're so brown all over, you're gorgeous." All the time tanning with my top off was worth it. He took off my shorts and kissed every part of me as my body danced with electricity and love. Quinn took off his shirt and I felt the smooth skin on his back as he pressed himself gently against me, his body hot and hard. I kissed the wolf tattoo on his right shoulder, felt his strong arms, kissed his lips which tasted like heat.

Quinn took off his pants and pulled a condom out from his wallet. He paused as his eyes searched my face. "You are so luscious, my Jezzy, is this okay, are you okay?"

"Yes, yes," I said. Quinn put on the condom and put himself in me gently first, then strong, fast. His moans turned louder and sounded like an animal, the wolf, and his green eyes were true and I whispered, "so good." I closed my eyes and held onto his back, then we flipped over and I was on top, his hands on my breasts as he exploded inside me.

I lay on top of him, our sweat and heat mixing like a cozy warm blanket. The radio played softly and my body was all tingles and alive. We rolled on our sides.

"You are so sexy," Quinn said. He kissed my lips and his fingers smoothed over my body, teasing, on my thighs and between my legs. His touch was light, rhythmic, he was kissing my neck and I couldn't hold on any longer and I had the best orgasm, shaking and laughing as he continued to touch me. Finally, it was too much, and I turned over, my head on his belly.

"Wow, wow," I said. His hands lingered on my back and we were still, breathing together, sticky with love.

Eric and I had discovered sex together when I was fifteen and he was seventeen. I didn't want to get pregnant so we used condoms, then I got an IUD which was weird and messed up my periods. We would spend hours atop his bed seeing how many orgasms we could give each other — I always won which he loved, he always wanted to 'do me one more time', tried different ways, with his hands, tongue, rubbing his penis against the best parts of me.

From the start sex made me feel something great, powerful,

connected, and with Quinn who held me tight and kissed my shoulders, I wanted this feeling to have permanence, have a home inside me.

Quinn got a towel and washed our sticky parts.

"Do you want a muffin? Lawrence is an amazing baker."

We sat on the mattress, ate muffins and drank lemonade.

Music from the radio was a woman with a lusty voice who sang with a piano and a guitar. "Who's that? She's so good."

"The one and only, Nina Simone."

"Wow, she's amazing. I want to play like her. That's blues, right?"

"Blues and jazz cross here and there, my sweet." He kissed me soft and long, chocolate chip muffin taste. The words Nina sang were about her man being gone. Outside, the day turned darker which put a sadness inside me knowing it was time for me to be gone. Mom panicked if we were off schedule and we had planned for departure at seven from our Newton house. My lips formed into a pout, I felt them move despite wanting the happy feeling.

Quinn stuck out his bottom lip. "Don't be sad, Jezebel."

"I'm not sad, my face is just sad."

"We will meet again, sweet Jezzy."

No promise, or plan, or tomorrow, just the sweet smell of him on my skin.

"I'll walk you to the train," Quinn said.

I shook my head. That empty feeling was already growing. I wanted his arms around me forever so I had to leave quick or I would seem desperate and needy. Nina sang 'Feelin' Good', we were happy, so it was time to go.

At the door, he picked up my tee-shirt, kissed my belly and with a black Sharpie wrote his number: 617-429-9958. I ran two blocks and caught the T.

As I sat there I knew I was tattooed with love which made that nagging beast called lonely sit across from me, not on my lap like it wanted.

CHAPTER EIGHT: PEACHES

I called Quinn two days later and Lawrence answered.

"Is Quinn there?"

"Me lady! He's on tour and sends you hugs and kisses."

"Okay, will he be back soon?" I hoped I didn't sound desperate.

"Yes, soon, a few weeks perhaps."

A few weeks! That would be in August with half the summer gone. It felt like an eternity. I gave Lawrence my number and hung up, yearning to feel Quinn's body wrapped around me, smell his cinnamon spice.

I decided that until he got back I would focus on getting a great tan and also, finding ways to get into the city. I had to start my piano lessons and was desperate to find Sparky and whatever club he was gigging at.

Dear Abby hadn't answered my letter yet and I kept checking the paper. I tried not to pay attention to my parents which wasn't hard, Dad was never here.

For the next two weeks I walked the beach, picked up shells and stones, and my body turned a deep brown with salt etched into my skin. Being with the ocean was hypnotic and peaceful and I started to meditate with instructions from the book I bought at George's Folly. It said to sit and focus on your breath and your mind will be still and peaceful, that when thoughts come up watch them as if they were passing clouds, letting them drift away as you focus back on the breath. At first I saw weird images behind my eyelids, my thoughts racing about Rachel, Quinn, piano, and everything else in my life. After a few minutes my mind became quieter, peaceful, and the ocean sounds in the background were soothing, the seagulls' cries song-like.

Every day at dusk I went to the beach and meditated and my insides turned calmer. Even when Mom's guy friends flirted with me with their wrinkled skin, overweight stomachs, squinty eyes and hopeful grins, I just smiled and pretended they weren't there. And mostly dealing with Mom was easier, especially since she was gone a lot with her new boyfriend. She rushed around with her routine of playing gin rummy or poker on various friends' porches, sunning on the beach, going to parties, all of it with a drink in her hand. Occasionally she would stop by my blanket on the beach and talk.

Like she did this morning.

I was starting to get restless being on the beach—missing Quinn missing my friends missing Rachel. Being connected with shells, sand, ocean, inner beings only goes so far and I felt edgy. Flipping through the meditation book, reading affirmations—today everything seemed trite, stupid.

Mom walked over to my blanket and sat on the edge. She had a plastic container of freshly cut peaches which she offered me and I took a few, chewing at the cool, sweet fruit that was smooth and crisp. Mom usually didn't come over to my area of the beach when she was with her friends so I wondered what was up. I munched on the peaches as she began to talk.

"Barry asked me to dinner tonight." She must have read something in my expression because she quickly added, "We're just friends, Jezebel."

"I didn't say anything."

"Still, I don't know if it's right, just him and I. What do you think?"

I think you should take me out to a lobster dinner and forget sleaze-ball Barry. But I didn't say that. Instead I quoted from the book I just read.

"Remember Your Worthiness." Mom looked at me and her blue eyes cleared like she was digesting what I said.

"You know you're right. I am worthy enough to go to dinner with Barry. I deserve to go out." She gave me an awkward sideways hug and got up "Thanks, darling." She turned, her thin, tan legs moving fast like a sandpiper, holding the empty plastic container with random peach juice in the corners.

I watched a small wave roll in over the sandbar signaling the start of high tide. Queasiness crept through my stomach from the peaches, or from Mom who had done something wrong with the wisdom I espoused. I wished I had said, "Take me for a lobster dinner, we don't need him," or something like that.

Worthiness. What was I worth? Didn't feel like much to Mom. I felt worthy when I was with Quinn. And playing the piano. And away from my family, on my own.

A bearded guy wearing a tie-dye shirt walked by smoking a joint and I almost followed him. Searching through my beach bag, I found the book by Timothy Leary, *The Psychedelic Experience*. I read a few paragraphs about acid trips, experiencing new realms of consciousness, and how to receive deep revelations.

That appealed to me. An LSD trip so I could get visions and messages. New realms of being. Change my course.

Wondering what advice someone like Timothy Leary would give me, I had the thought that he would answer a letter if I wrote him. And I could use my stationary with the peace signs.

Later that day I wrote and mailed the letter.

Dear Dr. Timothy Leary,

Hello, how are you?

Your address was in "The Psychedelic Experience", which I am enjoying reading. Since you are a psychologist and seem pretty smart and cool, I was wondering if you could advise me. My family is messed up. I'm sixteen almost seventeen, going to be a senior in High School. Mom drinks all the time and has a boyfriend even though her and my dad are still married. My dad did something weird and my sister and mom didn't believe me, they think I'm a big fat liar (I'm not fat). I want to run away with a band and be a piano player. Maybe we could meet in Harvard Square and talk?

Please write back soon.

Peace and Love, JB

CHAPTER NINE: BAYSIDE

It was kismet, fate, a gift!

I was invited to an LSD party bayside. Eric had called this morning. "Greyson's family rented a house on the bay, his parents sailed to Nantucket so we have the whole place to ourselves."

Acid trips equaled insight, revelations, vision quests, things I so desperately needed. Having just written to Dr. Timothy Leary yesterday, having read about all his great experiences, now I, Jezebel, was going to uncover boundless truths, answers to my million questions. I said I wanted to change my course. Here was my chance.

The atmosphere for acid trips was important, and as I rode my bike to the bay, I knew this house would be ideal. There was the quiet lapping of water by white wooden docks, moored boats swaying with the slight waves, low tide with plenty of clam shells, and the gulls dancing above as the sun set towards Boston. Leaning my bike against a wrap-around weather-beaten porch, a bird swooped past me, headed to sea. It joined some friends, hovered above the boats. Stars were beginning to light up the sky.

Welcoming people at the front door was Grey. I knew him from elementary school, he was a grade above, my sister's age of eighteen. He was permanently spaced out, even without drugs, just happy and in a cloud, and not caring about much. He came from a very wealthy family with five kids and always seemed to be shirtless and barefoot, humming a Grateful Dead song. Everyone got happy when they saw Grey. You could tell him anything, pour your heart out to him, only thing was after a few minutes you'd realize he had no idea what you were talking about and wasn't really listening, was just happy to breathe your air, feel your closeness. His skin was smooth with no blemishes, his hair was brown, long, silky soft which everyone knew because he made you feel it, he was skinny and seemed to only eat sour candies, no real food.

"Yes wow yes, it's Jezebel," Grey said, grinning widely. We hugged as he stuck his hand in a fish bowl and extracted a small square of paper. This LSD was blotter acid, dropped on little squares with pictures of tiny peaches for the Allman Brothers album, *Eat a Peach*.

"Lick the paper," Grey said.

A slight panic passed through me. Was this okay, how would it turn out? There were moments in past trips where things turned scary. But this night was different, I told myself. Everything was perfect. I licked the peach which was tasteless and the paper melted on my tongue with remnants by my teeth which I chewed.

"Come on in," Grey said.

Friends from Newton were hanging out in the living room. Good company was essential for acid trips, and I liked everyone there, knew everyone, except a couple of guys from Cambridge—a cute, tall Asian guy with long, straight black haired, thick framed black glasses named Jon, and a chubby, short Black guy named Larry who looked about ten-years-old but said he went to MIT. Eric was there, Cindy who used to be pretty but chopped off her hair, got fat and said she was now a lesbian, Missy who was ethereal with wispy yellow hair, dull blue eyes, going into senior year like me, and a really good artist with pencils and watercolors.

Grey put his arm around Larry. "Larry here will be our sober pilot for the evening."

Larry had a bottle of Heineken in his right hand and raised it, nodding hello. Cindy, Missy and Eric were sitting on a big, comfy couch with lots of fluffy, blue and white striped pillows. Two strobe lights flashed across the room, three tall drippy candles sat on a wooden table with a big mirror leaning against it. Someone had thrown a beach towel across the mirror which was smart—looking in a mirror on an acid trip is a bad idea since you can see every pore, vein, even the blood running through. Awful.

A huge Persian rug covered a dark wooden floor, bean bag chairs were around the room and bowls of popcorn, potato chips, red hots and bubble gum were placed on side tables.

I handed Greyson five dollars from a white envelope, for the acid.

"Why the envelope?"

"Grandma Bubbie," I said.

Grey and I shared a bean bag chair and watched candles flicker. As time passed, my fingers started to tingle and as I waved them, colorful trails followed in the air. Grey noticed them too and pointed, tracing them with his finger.

"All true species are here before us," I said, my voice sounding hollow.

"Infinity," said Grey as he pointed upward, holding his hands towards my face with stars shooting out of his fingertips. Atoms around my arms breathed, they too changed into red yellow green ribbons which made me move around, my body light as air.

The couch was no longer lifeless, it swayed as a boat might. It carried Eric and Missy who were entwined with no edges. Eric pulled me over onto his lap and kissed me on my mouth, a strange buzzing sensation emanated from his lips, not unpleasant.

"You've been eating roses," I said, falling into his eye sockets which were vast oceans.

Cindy sat next to Missy, pointing above as they focused on some imaginary movie, connected, no space between them, a double person. Who were they, really? One or many? I stood pondering as Jeff took off his shirt. His ribs protruded, they were branches of a tree extended with treasures. I touched his skin and he laughed and moved his limbs, creating trails of leaves. There was tree sap, or his blood that moved through his arms. We danced together as *Not Fade Away,* my favorite Dead song, coursed through the speakers.

Now wearing only underpants Grey stood tall and gave a lecture, his finger raised by his eyes.

"Melons are the utmost foremost fruit of fifteenth century Europe. I traveled far and wide and each new castle presented me with one hundred of these luscious specimens, gifts from kings." His laugh was rhythmic, notes sprayed from his mouth that kept a beat, "ha ha ha …"

I presented him with a melon. "In honor of your journey," I said.

"Thank you, my queen." Grey bowed low.

A light grew before me. "I am Queen Jezebel of the desert winds, a truth teller from ancient times." The story of the strength and alluring powers of Queen Jezebel that I had read at George's Folly had stayed with me. Now she and I were one.

"Here to serve you, my queen." Grey's head was nodding, bouncing, multiplying, merging with my body which was liquid. Stillness wasn't possible. I rolled to the carpet and watched a line of caterpillars crawl slowly, methodically across a red meadow.

"Amy, you have caterpillars," I might have said.

Grey hovered, now taller, a giant. "Amy's not here, my queen, only her thoughts."

Cindy stood next to me. A sharp unpleasant hiss pierced me as she whispered in my ear. "If you are Queen Jezebel you have power and strength beyond humans, you see truth." She pulled me closer, her words a river gushing in my brain. "Are you a truth teller? Are you?"

Cindy's last words echoed, "Are you, are you, are you…"

"Yes, I've been trying to tell them…" but Cindy was gone, a swirl of color.

An old wooden upright piano was nestled far back against a wall with a straight back chair and I crossed the room, side-stepping puffy clouds that had appeared.

"Presenting Jezebel, jazz piano player," I announced. I played along with the music that blasted out of the speakers. I was a maestro! I was Billie, the Duke, I was George Gershwin! My playing made a river of delicious sounds. When the song ended and I bowed. Thousands applauded.

Everyone was looking up at the ceiling except Grey who was eating licorice in the middle of the room, grinning. The front door was open and I walked out. There were shooting stars in a very black sky and the boats were rocking on the water. Larry followed me across the street to the steps that led down to the dark, still water of the bay. All was quiet except wind through sails and the lapping of small waves on the rocks, flap flap, splash. On the last step, I took off my sneakers, shorts and tee and stood in my bikini, a sensual breeze tingling my skin.

"Hey!"

Prancing across the street were Grey, Eric and Missy, naked, their bodies glowing, shimmering as they moved towards me. Together we stepped over rocks that shone with crystals and fell into the dark bay. As we swam the seagulls watched as a quiet hush, rocked by slow waves, embraced us. Minutes or hours passed as we floated.

When we emerged Larry was there with towels, warm pastel colored fabric that scratched at my skin. Missy took my hand as we walked, my clothes and sneakers lost, Missy singing a song to mermaids, her voice sweet and soft. Inside Larry handed me my clothes and as I put them on over my wet bathing suit I noticed Cindy standing by a picture of an Indian man, deep in conversation. I walked over and she turned, her mouth with too many lips.

"His Holiness the Dalai Lama, kindness, compassion, truth," she said. "A discussion here of which path is righteous, one of academic knowledge or practical application, a journey to the far east, perhaps."

His face looked strange, kind of like my grandma Bubbie. "He's my Bubbie," I said. His lips were moving and I wondered what message he was giving. "Does he expound knowledge?"

Cindy's head grew as she nodded and I moved away, everything suddenly too close, confusing, sharp. I yearned for something familiar, like cool clean air, a fog horn. My bike. I walked to the yard and Larry followed, watching me roll my bike to the street.

"You're okay to ride? Want me to walk you?"

His face was distorted, nose slanted into ear, not scary though, friendly. Feelings of intense love filled me and I put my bike down and hugged Larry. Words stuck on my teeth and disappeared. "I'm good," managed to escape and I watched the words blow away.

"Queen Jezebel of desert winds," Grey called from the porch, having followed us.

The idea that Grey knew who I was made that feeling of love intensify. All the strength of Queen Jezebel was mine. This was my revelation! Whatever happened, that power would be inside me. As I hugged Grey I knew this was the truth. On my bike I rode past dark houses with no streetlights, only the stars and sky guiding me home.

At home everything was quiet. Mom was still out, it was so late, almost morning? As I lay in my bed images of the night floated by. Greyson as a tree, Bubbie as the Dalai Lama, Eric's lips, Larry and the towels. The jazz piano concert I played. Images of Queen Jezebel, her red lips, my own face. Then a fire storm of fear began.

What answers did I receive, really? Who was I, even? Queen Jezebel, was she sneering at me? Fast and rough the questions shot at me like bullets, and in the darkness of the night in my room, Queen Jezebel appeared surrounded by fire, a sparkling crown perched on her head, her thick hair like snakes. Smiling, reassuring, yes there is truth, my child. I felt comforted until her smile cracked open too wide, blood pouring from her gums, terrible.

I hid under my covers and she was there, dark holes instead of eyes.

"This is the acid trip don't be scared," I told myself, yet my hands started to shake, my whole body wired. I ran from my room, turned lights on as the walls of my house melted. I needed someone, desperately. Please I'm scared, what do I do? My bike was on the porch and I ran out. Cool foggy air greeted me as I felt Aragorn's handlebars. Please comfort me, Aragorn. Thick layers of fog rolled in and I stood by my bike willing the fear away, every limb of my body brittle, alert.

Three figures walked through the haze, a dull yellow glow, blurred around their edges. Ghosts! As they moved closer I crouched behind my bike. Their shadows moved to my lawn and stopped.

"This is her house?" A deep growl, they were here, this was the end of me.

"Yes, although it's shaped oddly tonight." Eric.

I rose from my perch and Larry jumped. "What the heck?"

Eric, Larry and Cindy approached as the fire in my head simmered. "I got scared," I said, as they surrounded me with hugs.

"We were concerned," Larry said. "Cindy told us…"

Cindy put her hand on my cheek, she was pretty again, smooth skin and bright, nice eyes. "His Holiness the Dalai Lama told me at the end of our conference to follow you, not leave you alone. He gave me instructions."

We sat on my front steps, silent, my head against Cindy's shoulder. Sometime early morning the fog horn sounded, its pattern soothing. Fear floated away, my friends walked back, and I climbed into bed, finally drawn toward an acid filled sleep full of oceans, rocks, colors, and echoes.

CHAPTER TEN: FRIED CLAMS LUNCH

Eyelashes stuck, fluttered. I tried opening them. Light showed through the curtains that rustled in a warm breeze. My body felt stiff as I climbed out of bed wearing the same clothes as last night, everything damp, my mind hazy and clogged. The hangover from acid was unique, not like booze or speed, it was spacey with an irritable edge. Even breathing was annoying.

Had I received answers, insights from my acid trip? Be strong like Queen Jezebel who had scared me so much? She was sneaky, alluring, she bewitched me. Was I like that, did I want those qualities of cunning, fierce, intense? Mean?

My thoughts were slow and I stared at my bed, confused. I walked into the hall. The whole house was quiet, Mom's door was open and her room was empty. Outside was a sunny warm day, the first Sunday in August. I walked to the beach, hoping to get rid of the fog in my head, burning my feet on the hot pavement. The beach was crowded with lots of families, couples, umbrellas, coolers. The smell of suntan lotion was strong and there was a low mumble of the Red Sox game on a radio. Frisbees whizzed in the air.

On the sand, I veered right. Mom sat with her crowd at her spot, a drink in one hand, cards in the other, wearing a flowered one piece I hadn't seen before. She was with Barry and a few other guys playing cards as two fat women in huge hats looked on. My stomach twisted in a knot. Watching Mom have a good summer was so frustrating. Laugh away, Mom. I almost lost my mind last night, your husband has disappeared. Ha ha, Mom, enjoy yourself with fake teeth ugly man.

My head dripped sweat just seeing Mom, Barry and the fat ladies. I threw off my shorts and tee, ran into the ocean and dove under a wave as cool refreshing water washed over me. I floated over white foam from a break, watched seagulls, felt an undertow pull, tasted salt on my lips. Most days the ocean and sun made me happy yet today as I walked to the shore, my body felt unsettled and achy, my brain still hazy from the acid.

I stood and gazed at boats far off.

Today, Dad was supposed to come for our annual fried clam's lunch with Bubbie. Bubbie didn't enjoy the beach anymore, said too many people made her feel overheated. She never missed her clam's lunch, though. Dad was picking her up in Brookline, they'd drive here, get me and we'd eat by Paragon Park at the esplanade. Mom had begged off, said she didn't feel well. Watching her with her friends, it sure looked like she felt okay.

After staring at the ocean and thinking about nothing, I walked back and sat on the front steps. Dad picked me up in his Oldsmobile at noon with Bubbie in the passenger seat. New car smell greeted me. Dad traded his car every two years getting the same exact car but an updated model.

The clam shack was five minutes from my house. It was a weather-beaten counter on the boardwalk that had fantastic clams—fat bellied, crisp, rich. There was table service, young people with summer jobs. Our picnic table was clean with napkins, plastic utensils, Heinz Ketchup bottles, mustard containers, salt and pepper.

"Look at all the seagulls," Bubbie said as she pointed to an overflowing garbage can. She wore a thin house dress that was faded green and looked about fifty years old. Next time the dress man Nathan was on the beach, I'd buy her a new dress, they weren't expensive. Nathan walked the beach with armfuls of dresses selling to the ladies—rumor was he put his three kids through college with the money he made. Mom called them 'Shmatte's', Yiddish for 'rag', but everyone loved Nathan and bought his dresses.

I remembered that last night I thought the Dalai Lama and Bubbie looked alike, but now I saw the only thing they had in common was the shape of their heads. Maybe that was the message. Bubbie is my answer.

Two kids on bikes charged the seagulls and they scattered, one grabbing a half-eaten ear of corn. A waiter came to our table who was blond, tan, cute, muscular with no shirt and jean shorts.

"Three fried clams, three lemonades," Dad said.

The waiter smiled at me as he gave us water in plastic cups.

"That's cool, no shirts. I like that," I said.

He winked. "Working outside, baby, the only way."

When he left Bubbie took my hand. "All the boys like you, bubelah." She turned to Dad. "Such pretty daughters you have, Saul."

Dad glared at me.

Another set of seagulls landed by the garbage, surfers walked past with boards under their arms and different songs from two radios crossed vibrations. Our food came, delivered by a tan girl wearing a bright, yellow sundress. We ate in silence, Bubbie focusing on the clams, pushing away her fries. They were such delicacies, sweet meat inside, salty outside, and mine were soon gone.

Bubbie put hers in front of me. "I've had enough."

"Dad, want some?" He shook his head so I finished Bubbie's clams.

Bubbie said, "Saul, you took vacation?"

Dad was facing the ocean and gazed above her head. "A few days, Ma. It's my busy season."

"You work too much. He used to be a ballplayer, your father, minor league, did you know that, Jezebel?"

I nodded. "How come you stopped, Dad?"

His gaze stayed far away. "We were poor and hungry. I had to make money."

Bubbie patted his hand. "Lefty they called him. Those were difficult years." She stood, using the table for balance. "I have to use the toilet at the house."

Back at the house when Bubbie was using the toilet, Dad stopped me as I was getting my beach bag. "You're too friendly," he said.

"What? What do you mean?"

"At the restaurant with the waiter. Men get the wrong idea. Don't be so friendly." He wagged his finger in my face.

"I was just talking, Dad." This was stupid, I didn't do anything.

"Take some lessons from your sister. She's appropriate, not a flirt."

That stung. I wasn't a flirt. Only with guys who liked me or kidding around with friends. Dad was being weird and my acid hangover had me especially testy.

"Sure you want me to take lessons from Rachel? She's pregnant, you know."

His mouth dropped and an expression I'd never seen before appeared on his face. Before I had a chance to back away he slapped me, hard. I turned, my reflexes were good, all those years playing sports. The impact hit my right ear and the side of my head started throbbing.

"I'm ready." Bubbie shuffled into the room, unaware. She took my hand and hugged me. "Come by soon, I have more pictures."

Without a glance at Dad, I hugged Bubbie, grabbed my towel on the porch, and stormed off.

People were gathered at the water's edge with skim boards, chairs, waders standing ankle deep. I dodged people and kicked water. My toe stung with salt water that entered a cut, my body felt weird and now my ear hurt.

I didn't understand, was Dad jealous?

Last year he took me to a movie, *The Last Picture Show*. Watching it with him was uncomfortable. The story was about a high school student who had an affair with the coach's wife. Dad had put his arm around me and moved his hand on my boob, right there in the movie. I shook his arm away, stuffed popcorn in my mouth and vowed never to see another movie with him for as long as I lived.

Most summers Rachel was here for Bubbie's clam lunch and things ran smoothly, so this was her fault. My stomach felt heavy and I didn't know what to do. Run, scream, swim until I couldn't breathe? Watch minnows, eat a minnow, kill a minnow? Those sweet little innocent creatures?

Far at sea three speed boats whizzed by. A barge moved slowly on the horizon. I will swim to you, barge, hop aboard, sail away.

Something hard banged my ankle. "Ow!"

A girl with a bright pink boogie board had bumped into my leg. She was about eight, with curly brown hair and a red polka-dot bikini, pudgy.

"Sorry!" She flung her hair from her eyes and ran back for another wave. I spotted a piece of brown sea-glass and grabbed it. It was old and smooth with orange hues. I palmed it, waded towards a set of waves and dove under the first one. Green ocean numbness touched my skin. Salt, foam splashed my face. When I popped up the boogie board girl was with two other girls laughing and talking, all wearing polka dot bikinis, one blue and white, the other orange and white.

"Want a ride?" Her friends paddled over and she slid her board towards me.

"Hey, thanks." A set of three waves were coming and I grabbed one, pumping my legs to the perfect spot right before it broke. Currents pushed me, smooth and fast. At the shore rocks and pebbles scraped my feet and I lay there letting water wash over me.

The girls seemed flattered that a cool teen was using their board. Red and white polka dot asked, "What's your name?"

"Jezebel."

"That's pretty. I'm Pearl, this is Donna, and that's Liza. You can take another ride if you want."

I rode another wave, this one slower and lingering. I started to feel better even with a corner of my mind scratching at some recent bruise.

"Thanks so much."

Pearl said, "Hey we'll see you tomorrow, we're here for all of August."

Tide was high and people were leaving, the lovers of late afternoon beach light hunkering down, reveling. Mom was still at the beach with Barry, her back towards me, the fat ladies gone. I felt angry that she missed lunch. I planned on telling her Dad hit me. She'd ask why and what would I say? He said I was flirting? Mom always flirted. She was charming, funny, a good artist and all but I wished she was more like our neighbor Edith. Just a mom to give me advice and tell me that mistakes were a part of life, that I'd be okay.

I put my towel around my neck and hurried off the beach. I had to phone Rachel and tell her about saying she was pregnant. Dad probably didn't believe me or maybe he did and that's why he hit me or maybe he hit me because of the clam lunch. Nothing made sense. The meditation book advised, "Think Positive Thoughts", so I forced myself. Whispering, I said all the things I wished for: "Quinn, Sparky, truth. Quinn, Sparky, truth. Quinn, Sparky, Quinn."

My new piece of sea glass was nestled in my palm.

CHAPTER ELEVEN: NIXON'S RESIGNATION

Amy called from Maine a few days later. "Come with me to look at Smith College. I'm going Friday."

College. Unopened catalogs sat next to my shell collection. My parents hadn't said anything, my guidance counselor, an old lady with a disappointed mouth, shook her head and told me to retake the SAT's. I wished I was going to college this fall with Rachel. I didn't want to be stuck at home alone with the parents.

"Okay," I told Amy. "I'll check out the other colleges, like UMASS." We made plans for Amy to pick me up at the ferry.

Thursday August 8, the day before we went, Mom's political friends visited. Chip and Henri came to the house talking furiously about Nixon and some impending news. Henri wore a flowered shirt and white shorts and Chip wore blue surfer shorts and a striped tee. Mom surprised me by inviting me to sit with everyone on the beach. I liked Chip and Henri. They didn't tease, they listened when I spoke and talked to me normally, not in that jokey way the other college kid Alan did. Henri had brought a picnic lunch, gourmet foods from Harvard Square. Mom must have told Barry that she had friends visiting because he was nowhere in sight.

Chip sat in a beach chair grinning at the ocean as he dug his feet in the sand, pale in his blue surfer shorts and no shirt. "First time at the beach this summer, it's about time you invited us, Sylvie." He spread baby oil over his arms and chest.

I shook my head. "Chip, you're going to burn." He pointed to his hat which hung a shadow over his face.

Henri had brought a feast— French bread, brie, olives, assorted fancy meats including prosciutto, cherry tomatoes, hard pears, fancy lemonade, pastries including small French meringues. He brought real plates that were bright yellow and green—summertime colors.

No one had cocktails which surprised me. During lunch Henri raised his glass of lemonade. "Let's toast Nixon's resignation."

I almost dropped my glass; I knew this was pending at some point but hadn't watched the news lately. "What, when?"

Chip said, "Tonight at 9:00."

"We'll watch," Mom said. "Jez, this is history in the making." She spread brie on her bread. "His resignation is long overdue, that bastard."

"Now we'll be stuck with Ford." Chip made a face.

"Nixon's a crook, we should have impeached him when Watergate broke." Henri cut up a pear and I took a piece.

They talked politics for a while and I listened, a warm breeze floating through the air. Henri, Chip and I took a swim as Mom watched by the shore—she was afraid of deep water and would only go up to her ankles and pat water on her arms.

When we finished our swim, Mom handed me three small shells. "For your collection." This version of Mom was so great; relaxed and caring. I knew I had to be careful since any minute she could change. Still, it felt nice.

Later at our house we barbecued steaks and hot dogs, piled food on our plates and gathered around the television to watch Nixon's resignation speech. Nixon wore a dark blue suit, white shirt, blue tie.

He exuded defeat as he read his speech from white pieces of paper, his cufflinks shiny.

When he said, "I no longer have a strong enough political base in the Congress to justify continuing that effort..." Henri yelled, "Understatement of the year!"

Vice President Ford was getting sworn into office tomorrow when I was off to Amherst with Amy. In pain from his sunburn, Chip didn't say much. Mom rubbed aloe lotion on his arms and back and I didn't say, "I told you so," even though I wanted to.

In the middle of Nixon's resignation speech, I called Rachel.

"Rachel! Are you watching this?" I heard Nixon's voice in her room and people chattering.

"I know, he had this coming! Jez, there's tons of people here, I'll call you tomorrow."

"Miss you Rachel."

"Miss you too, Jez."

I hung up and stared at the TV. Nixon was talking about goals of peaceful nations and how he ended America's longest war, Vietnam, all the work still ahead and how he wished he could finish his term.

I drifted outside remembering images from the Vietnam war and all the protests, how there were so many casualties from that stupid war. It was funny, my parents were so concerned about ending wars and creating a peaceful nation yet didn't seem to know how to stop fighting with each other.

After Nixon's speech, I kissed everyone goodnight and went to bed feeling hopeful about changes that were happening in the country and maybe in my own life. I had a cute, musician boyfriend, a music teacher named Sparky somewhere in Boston, and tomorrow, a road-trip with my best friend Amy.

CHAPTER TWELVE: THREE ANTS

In the morning Mom drove me to Pemberton to catch the ferry which was a quick twenty-five minutes to Boston. As I stood on the top deck of the ferry, my hair blew furiously in the wind. We motored past small islands, sailboats, and low flying planes headed to Logan Airport. The ocean spray felt fantastic on my face. It was hot and humid and I wore a flannel shirt over my knit bikini top with short shorts. A bunch of kids from a camp who wore the same blue tee-shirts that said, "Kawana" were grouped together, holding onto the rail next to me.

"We're going to the aquarium to see fishes," said a little girl around eight-years-old wearing a flowered sundress, her hair in pigtails. I nodded and smiled as I took off my shirt, wrapping it around my waist. A boy next to her stared at my boobs so I wrapped my flannel shirt around my neck with the arms hanging over my chest.

Amy met me with her mom's silver Cadillac and we hit the road. She talked about the colleges she wanted to visit and that Smith was on top of that list. After that we listened to Janis Joplin and Grace Slick, singing at the top of our lungs.

At the corner of Main and South Pleasant Streets in Amherst, Amy and I made plans to meet at 4:30. The air was sticky, hot and humid—a great beach day. Whenever I was anywhere else except the beach I always wished I was there.

Music was coming from the town common and I crossed over and stood next to a lawn sign announcing "Amherst Concert Series." The sounds of a fiddle, banjo and mandolin filled the air.

I bought a vanilla milkshake from a food stand which advertised *From Local Cows*.

"Best ice cream in western mass," said a cute guy who was leaning against the table.

"Thanks, George, you're my best advertisement," the stand guy said. They continued their conversation and I roamed around for a place to sit and listen. There was a patch of grass near a blanket with hippies and I plopped down.

"Hey, join us." A guy from the hippie blanket beckoned me over, while a woman with tiny braids in her hair offered me some weed. I walked over and accepted the weed, taking a deep toke. Someone on my other side passed me a jug of Boones Farm Apple wine.

The bluegrass band ended and another band started playing rock. Weed kept circulating and I started feeling buzzed. Everyone was dancing so I got up too. The woman took my hand and spun me around; I fell into a pile of dirt and we both laughed as she helped me to my feet. Surprisingly she kissed me on the lips and it felt really soft and nice.

There was a break in the music. I sat, grabbed some stale bread and warm mushy cheese, and started to feel anxious. The sun hid behind fast-moving clouds as everything turned grey. My mind was confused from weed and wine, my mouth cheesy and dry. I took another swig of warm, sweet wine and felt thirstier and a bit sick.

I suddenly remembered my purpose for being here. "Where's UMASS?"

The woman who had kissed me pointed down the main street. "About two miles that way." She nodded to the neat, brick buildings across from the common. "That's Amherst College."

Standing, I saw a tidy, white stone building on the corner that said "Lord Jeffery Inn", beyond which were beautiful green lawns and buildings that appeared both old and well-kept. At least I didn't have to lie when the guidance counselor asked me if I had seen any colleges.

Another joint was passed around which I indulged in. It was stupid because my brain was already so foggy. The heat was oppressive, thick and sticky and I wished I was on my beach blanket reading Siddhartha with a sea breeze. Amy was supposed to drop me back at my beach house, but time had gotten away.

"Does anyone know what time it is?"

A guy with a blond ponytail and no shirt sang, "Does anybody know what time it is, does anybody really care?" A few people laughed as the next band started playing, five minutes went by or an hour, I was too stoned and everything was slow-motion.

I grabbed my bag and went to a candy booth where the man was packing up and he told me it was 5:00.

"That couldn't be right," I said, panicked.

Slow down, heart, breathe in deep, breathe out long. I asked someone else and he removed a pocket watch from his vest with a big, long chain. "5:00, my dear," he said, his mustache smiling.

Panicked, I ran back to where Amy said to meet. She wasn't there or anywhere; it was too late and there went my ride home. How did that happen? My head was scrambled with that disgusting cheap wine and weed. Sweat was dripping down my back and my knees had clumps of dirt on them. Amherst was Massachusetts and so was my beach house yet they were three hours apart. Was there a bus, a train? Hitchhike? Could I ask that woman for help? Flies zipped towards my face, drinking my salty sweat.

Back at the blanket everyone was dancing again. They passed me wine and I didn't want any of the warm sweet liquid, like the sweat dripping down my back. Through the haze that was my mind I searched for clarity, an idea, something helpful.

"Loosen up, chicky," said the hippie guy as he waved his hands in front of my face. I wanted to punch him and say, you fucking smiling dirty hippie scumbag, give me a ride home if you're so free. The woman who was my sort of friend had disappeared.

The music was some original rock that was loud and bad. Old hamburger smell filled the air and everything breathed like hot grease.

Queen Jezebel was strong, confident, fearless. She would know what to do. Queen Jezebel, my namesake, please give me strength, clarity.

I wandered away from the hippie blanket. My head throbbed and I needed water. The man who I saw earlier by the ice cream stand stood by a tree watching me. Was that a sign? He was twenty-five or older with medium-length brown hair, cute, and clean looking. He seemed nice before and if he was from around here he might know of a swimming hole. And if I got up the courage, I could ask about a ride home. Or partway. Something.

I took a step toward him with half a smile.

He called to me, his voice clear and friendly. "Are you enjoying the concert?"

I nodded and walked closer. He wore khaki hiking shorts and his blue tee said UMASS Amherst. Most likely a professor. Yes, this would work.

Even though I felt like I was going to faint, I stood straight and pointed to his shirt. "UMASS, I was going to tour that school except I came here instead."

"It's a good college," he said with a grin.

"Do you know of a swimming hole near here?" I pointed to my dirty knees. "I need to get clean and this heat is gross."

He looked me up and down which made me take one step back, but then said in a clipped, strong professor voice, "I live by UMASS and if you want you can use my shower and on the way, see the college. I can drive you back here."

That sounded reasonable. Still, there was a little voice that whispered, *No, Jezebel.*

Someone on stage started a loud drum solo and the grease in the air thickened. I'd go with the professor, take a quick shower and if he was really nice I'd ask him for a ride to Boston. That way I wouldn't have to take my chances hitchhiking.

"Okay, I'm meeting my friend here soon so a ride back sounds great." A friend Amy, who was most likely halfway to Boston. I held out my hand. "My name's Jezebel."

He recoiled and a shadow crossed his face when I said my name, then it changed to a quick smile.

"George." His handshake was limp and sweaty which somehow gave me more courage, and I followed him to the street, getting in his grey pickup with a UMASS sticker on his window. We drove past the college and massive huge towers came out of nowhere amidst corn fields and farm land, which he said were dorms. Beside them were brick buildings, sports fields— a massive spread—way too big. I liked the lay-out of Amherst College better.

Right after UMASS he turned down a long dirt road surrounded by corn fields. At the end was a small wooden house with a front porch, tidy yard, with another huge corn field in back that seemed to go on forever. Shadows deepened and trees around his house swayed in a sudden wild wind, threatening a storm.

We parked and I followed him. "What do you teach at UMASS?" My mouth was dry with a metallic taste and my stomach was in knots. Being away from the music and crowds felt scary and his house was isolated. I reached for my flannel shirt and it wasn't there, lost somewhere in the haze of the day.

As we walked in the front door he said, "I'm no professor, I work in food services." He said this with intensity as if it was a much more important job, though in my mind I pictured the ladies with aprons and sweaty pink faces who doled out food at our high school cafeteria, complaining and angry at us for being privileged.

He led me down a hall and through a clean, tidy kitchen to the back of the house where there was a small bathroom with a glass enclosed shower next to a sink. There was a fresh bar of soap with some potpourri in a dish. There was probably a girlfriend who lived here because the bathroom was sparkling clean. Still, I didn't relax. I'd shower fast and leave. This was not a good idea, yet I felt unable to stop.

"Have a beer with me before you shower." As I stood in the hall he handed me a can of Budweiser. "What a son-of-a-bitch hot day." He opened his beer and took off his shirt, his chest coated with black hair with a fat, white belly hanging over his khaki shorts, sweat dripping from his body which made his chest hair look similar to a carpet. I stared, mesmerized, then looked away quickly, my stomach churning.

"Too bad about Nixon, huh?"

My breath caught and I started to choke. I chugged some beer which was cold and tried not to look at this person who's house I was in, who I was at the mercy of.

"Yeah, George, really, best president ever."

He tilted his head, unsure, not catching the sarcasm in my voice that I somehow couldn't contain.

"I'll just shower fast," I said. "My friend expects me back soon."

The bathroom door had no lock. I took off my sneakers, bathing suit and shorts, stuck them by the door and climbed in the shower. The cool water was refreshing although I felt panicked. I washed fast, drank from the stream, turned the water off and dried myself with a grubby towel. When I threw on my shorts and top I looked around for a weapon, anything sharp. From his backyard birds chirped loudly around a bird feeder and there was a broken-down shed, dark and foreboding. The bathroom door handle rattled and I froze.

"Be right there," I said, my voice high and frantic.

Sneakers in my hand, I leaned hard against the door. He pushed it and I pushed back. "One sec," I said.

His next push threw me against the wall. "Where'd you go?" he said as he entered.

He was naked and stood by the sink, his eyes on my body, greedy.

Siddhartha came upon many obstacles and handled them with courage and strength. He encountered demons, monsters, the darkest of nights. Jezebel killed false prophets, protected her followers, did whatever was necessary.

The guy moved toward me, his breath heavy with beer and sex. "I knew you wanted this as soon as I saw you." He pressed his erection against my hip and I pushed him, hard.

"Wrong!" I slid out to the hallway, almost slipping on a puddle of water, innocent on the floor.

He followed me, enraged now, his palms open, bewildered. "What the fuck is this?"

The air was still. Cars drove by too far away, corn fields swayed, clouds passed over the sun, dark shadows bounced off the wall and I was frozen, trapped. This was happening.

He stood too close. "What kind of game is this? You're in my house, away from everyone, I could rape you, kill you! No one would know, you stupid girl." Spit rolled down his chin as he yelled and I shook my head, tears filling my eyes.

A siren wailed somewhere close and it startled him, confusing his mission. As I backed up he glared at me. "Get in my truck, I'll take you to Amherst because I'm a nice guy." He turned and walked into another room and I ran out the back door. No way was I getting in his truck.

His backyard was quiet, the only sound birds, they seemed to squawk at me, run, dumb girl, run! I ducked and ran past his side windows, ran through his yard towards the corn field, stones tearing at my feet, corn stalks ripping my body.

His front door slammed and I ran faster.

He was furious, rage apparent. "You fucking girl, you better run!"

I didn't turn, just ran as fast as ever, 50-yard-dash from junior high school, I was the anchor leg, knew how to win a race. Through the cornfield the stalks were tall, corn unpicked, and scratches appeared on my legs, my stomach, red lines etched. The road was ahead. There were cars, people. Existence.

I ran across and sat on the shoulder, meadows and green fields behind me. My feet were bleeding and filthy, my legs and arms a mess of scratches. Lacing up my sneakers, I noticed a big, bloody cut on my left toe.

Three ants crawled across my knee. They were slow and friendly, taking their evening stroll. "Hi, ants," I said. "Help me." One of them stopped and seemed attentive, then continued along its way.

It was dusk, around six—people were headed to dinner, a concert, somewhere safe with friends, and I stuck out my thumb, my only way back. A green Volvo stopped and I ran over. A lady around forty with grey hair and round glasses said, "Amherst?"

In the car the lady focused on the road, scrunched down as if she just learned to drive, which was better for me because she didn't ask questions and we drove in silence. I took a tissue from the console and wiped off the blood from my scratches. She glanced at them and stared back at the road.

Outside seemed strangely lit with a red glow, some yellow wisps that intertwined, surreal. Soon we were at the common and the woman pulled the car over.

"Thank you," I said.

She waved and stared at the road, unmoving. Could this day get any stranger?

The sun had started to fade in a warm August vapor. My hippie friends had gone, musicians were scattered around packing up their things, and the air was thick with sweet incense. A strange group were dancing, they wore long burlap skirts, one person played a recorder, the others, cymbals. A little man brought up the rear, wearing purple robes playing a high pitched tuneless song on a penny whistle. They danced by me, in their dream or mine, round and around this troubadour went, and I imagined that man did kill me, and this was me being dead.

On a bench, I sat and put my legs up, wrapped my arms around myself, curled so I would wake up or go to sleep, not this half terrified numb state. The light was dim with the setting sun, oh, I had to get home, if this wasn't a dream and I wasn't dead, I would be in such trouble, grounded, smacked, screamed at by both parents separately, days apart, continuous.

Where were my answers now, where was the inspiration? Closing my eyes in hopes of clarity nothing came, only images of corn stalks, a farmhouse, face of the psycho man. Who would do that? I only wanted a shower, there was nothing wrong with that, was there? He offered. And he seemed nice, he was friends with the ice cream man.

A piano played somewhere across the green. Why hadn't I spent the day searching for Sparky? Instead I wasted it. Dumbness was what I possessed, not strength.

The piano was soothing in its melancholy and I found myself walking over. A tall man with a long black braid moved his hands over the keyboard while a woman with dreamy eyes stood next to him, tapping lightly on a tambourine.

He finished the song and smiled. "Do you play?" His voice was soft and kind.

Feeling suddenly exposed, my body too bare, I folded my arms, covering my stomach, and nodded. He seemed to notice and reached into a box, extracting a green sweatshirt which he handed to me.

"Looks like you didn't get one of these from the concert, here, I have extra."

Written on the back was, "Amherst Concert Series, 1974". It was big on me and covered even my shorts which I was happy about. My whole face felt heavy as this man's show of kindness brought a hunger and homeless feeling inside, and I stood unbalanced, unsure.

The woman handed him a cover for his keyboard and he whispered to her, after which he went about the business of packing up. The sun dipped, the day almost gone, everything paused.

She took a step toward me. "Are you okay, darling?" Her voice was sweet with concern and I couldn't hold my tears so they rained down my cheeks, my chest shaking with screams that wanted to escape. As I cried, she hugged me.

After a couple of minutes, I said, "It's just, someone was really mean. And I missed my ride." She nodded and I was happy she didn't ask any questions that I wouldn't be able to answer.

As I summoned up courage to ask about a ride, I heard my name across the common, or was that the high pitch of that penny whistle? I heard it again. "Jezebel!"

Was it the guy?

"Oh my God, Jez, I found you!" Amy ran across the common as tears ran down her cheeks. She hugged me so hard my arm scratches stung, her blond hair matted to her wet face.

"I'm so sorry, I can't believe you're still here!" She explained about a barbecue at Smith College, how she visited dorms, heard chamber music, forgot about the time, would I ever forgive her, she was two hours late and was so glad I was still here. Her lips moved fast, her face was beet red and I just prayed thank you to my guardian angel wherever you are.

The troubadours still circled with their endless dance as the piano man and woman packed their stuff. The woman said, "Good, your friend found you."

A wave of gratitude washed over me. "Thank you for being nice, for your help."

The woman handed me a flyer. "We play at Cambridge Common in a few weeks, you should come by, play a song if you'd like."

"Oh, wow, that would be great."

Amy pulled my hand to go, anxious to continue our reunion.

I stuffed the flyer in my bag. "Hey, do you give piano lessons?"

"Check us out in Cambridge, we'll talk."

Amy took my arm and led me from the common as I glanced back at the surreal scene, a blur of dust and heat. Daylight faded as we got in her car. Amy had stopped crying and talked a mile a minute about Smith College which she loved, the girls were so nice, classrooms were workshop style with chairs in a circle, the campus was beautiful. Her dialogue was marked with excitement and interspersed with apologizes. My body felt glued to the leather seat and I nestled into the green sweatshirt, put on the hood and leaned against the window.

"How was your day, Jez? You seem upset."

I considered telling her the truth, how I made a wrong turn, chasing something I wasn't even sure of. I glanced at her face, red with excitement, her eyes on the road as she sat tall with the success of her day. Amy was a good friend, a solid person, girl scout for many years, honorable. Loyal. I trusted her, and yet, couldn't risk telling her what happened. What if she thought it was my fault. Was it my fault? She might think I was stupid. Was I?

There was a pause as Amy waited for my answer, looking at me sideways with caring eyes. The happenings of the day were so full inside me, my body hurt and tears threatened to explode. I was grateful for the darkness inside the car.

"My day was strange, I mean, the heat was unbearable."

"I know, at the barbecue everyone was pouring sweat. Hey, are you hungry? Reach in my bag, I got snacks."

In her backpack were five little plastic bags, each with a different snack—popcorn, candy kisses, M&Ms, pretzels, chips. Someone had had the arduous task of picking different colored ribbons to close the bags. I pictured a bunch of Smith girls on a Sunday afternoon as they sat on a bench outside their dorm, sorting and tying as they laughed in the sun, talking about last night's dates.

Food. One bite salty, the next bite sweet. Delicious. I focused on textures.

"Thanks for bringing snacks, I only had a frappe and some disgusting wine. I saw Amherst College and UMASS, Amherst was better."

She munched a pretzel, her eyes on the road. "Smith students said UMASS is called "Zoo Mass.""

"Yeah, the campus is huge."

She nodded. "A smaller college would be better for you, Jez, so you don't get lost in the crowd. Even though you could never get lost in a crowd, you're too cool and original."

I reached over and squeezed her hand. She had so much faith in me, my friend. I didn't say there was no way I would apply to UMASS, didn't say the words I wanted to forget, describe the terror I felt.

"Anything else happen? Meet any cute guys?"

Dark eyes. Belly. Broken-down shed.

"Nah, just weirdos." I snuggled in my hoodie. "Except the couple you saw at the end, the guy gave me this sweatshirt."

Amy spoke of the courses Smith College offered and how she was going for early admission, how students had given her essay suggestions and tips about classes with favorite professors and which restaurants had good, inexpensive food. We rolled along the highway and her voice faded with the hum of tires as I drifted, half-asleep, images of strange characters, a too clean bathroom and those three ants, crawling across my knee.

CHAPTER THIRTEEN: THE BROTHERS

The next few days were rainy and I stayed in bed, sleeping my life away. No part of me wanted consciousness. My scratches stung, body ached, my brain stalled with bad images. Nothing to get up for. I hoped my life would change somehow without me doing anything. On the fourth day, the sun blasted through the curtains and I knew I had to take action. The summer was buzzing by; it was already August 13 and I still hadn't found Sparky. All I was doing was getting in trouble.

On the way to the bathroom I saw my knit bikini bathing suit top from yesterday in the corner of the floor. Dirt, sweat and shame encased in the fabric and I threw it in the garbage and went to shower.

Scrubbing hard, all the scum from Amherst running down the drain, I wanted the memory of that creep off my skin, out of my head. My stomach felt queasy and empty. I wrapped a towel around me and went to the kitchen, got a box of ginger snaps and a tall glass of milk which I drank in three seconds and ate half the box of cookies as I stood by the sink.

It was a beautiful day with a clear blue sky, and people pulled their carts with chairs, boogie boards and coolers towards the beach. The yappy dog walked by with a bigger friend, a labrador, both on a leash with their owner. I missed Quinn, needed him, and wished Rachel was here, someone to talk with. Dear Abby hadn't responded to my letter and no word from Timothy Leary either.

There was a new black bikini that I forgot about in my drawer. I put that on and was almost out the door when our phone rang. We had a new push button, sky blue phone with a cord that reached into the kitchen and was constantly tangled. It was fun to hold the chord up and watch it spin as, presto, it untangled. The ring was loud and surprised me since we hardly ever got calls at the beach house.

"Hello?"

"My sweet Jezebel."

"Quinn!"

"How's it going?"

"Great, I mean, okay, how are you?"

With my excitement, the phone slipped from my hand, bouncing on the floor. I chased it, afraid I would lose the connection.

"Hi, sorry! Where are you?"

"Home, and we're gigging in Provincetown. Want to come?"

"Yes, that's sort of near my beach house!" As he spoke with his smooth, sing-song voice I was pulled into the music world again. I pictured a dimly lit nightclub by the beach with a stage, Quinn playing with his band. This was perfect, something to erase the awfulness that had happened. I would be with Quinn! Quinn with his green eyes, smooth touch, and all the music.

He said we'd leave Friday morning between nine and eleven and return Sunday. Quinn didn't know I'd need permission. He was twenty-one or so and we hadn't spoken about our ages when we had our fun time together at his place. We hung up and I danced around the house, awed that just a few days ago I was saying his name over and over as my mantra and now we were going to be together.

Mom was an obstacle—I would have to make up a good story. I had to go, hanging with Quinn and his band was a dream come true and this was going to happen. Everything was coming together.

The hot pavement burned and I didn't even care. The beach was crowded, and I didn't see Mom at her usual spot, so I decided on a swim. Taking off my tee and shorts, I headed to the water. Two guys with muscles, tattoos and great tans were throwing a football, and they stared at me as I passed.

The guy holding the ball said, "Hi, gorgeous."

I smiled, waved and kept walking. The water was crystal clear cold from days of rain with low waves that rippled towards me, the perfect temperature for cooling your body. Standing beside me was a group of adults I recognized.

"Hi Jezebel, is your mother here today?" It was Edith who lived two houses down, was short and large, older than Mom, nosy, and always offered me candy or cookies every time she saw me on the porch. She'd yell from her lawn, "Come over, I just baked!" I would wave and say, "Can't!" and motion to my house as if I had chores. One summer I got stuck listening to her talk about nothing for an hour, framed pictures and glass menagerie staring at me as I ate so many cookies I felt sick.

"She's here somewhere." I waved and continued into the water, then dove under a white cap and felt the world disappear. Sounds muffled and everything was green. Popping up, I floated for a few minutes. Seagulls overhead watched for fish. Quinn had called, he called! His arms would soon be around me like this wave—comfort and love.

Avoiding neighbors, I made my way to the shore, dripping wet as I walked past the football guys.

One of them called, "What's your name?" I smiled and kept walking except slower.

"Okay, be that way," he said.

I stopped and he walked over, holding the football under his arm. He was tall and very handsome with neat, light-brown shaggy hair to his ears, bright blue eyes, rugged looking with a straight nose and a dimple on his chin. He had a few tattoos and one by his heart that said, "2/14/68 RIP Patrick".

"Come have a beer with us." He motioned to a big blanket with a blue cooler and two beach chairs. He seemed nice, we were in public and an ice cold beer sounded fantastic.

"Okay, I'll get my towel."

When I walked over, they were talking and stopped abruptly. The other guy offered me the chair which was a nice change from my towel, and handed me a bottle of Heineken. Classy. I needed to hone my ability to read people, see which guys were nice, which were creeps. I thought I was good at that until my big mistake last Friday with the fake professor.

Dimple guy held up his bottle. "Cheers." I took a sip of the cold, refreshing beer which was the best thing I had all day. He sat in a blue and white striped beach chair, a matching towel over its back. "I'm John and that's my brother Teddy."

On the blanket, Teddy opened up a bag of Wise potato chips. He had the same bright blue eyes as his brother, cheek dimples, and blond hair that was cut shorter than John's with a side part.

"Nice to meet you John and Teddy. Same as the Kennedys."

John laughed. "Yes, or a thousand other Boston Irish Catholic families with seven kids."

"I'm Jezebel."

John's eyes widened and his brows arched. "Wow, I don't hear that name much."

I shrugged. "She gets a bad rap but she was actually a strong, powerful woman."

They smiled and nodded and I was glad not to have to say more. I didn't think I could explain how much Queen Jezebel meant to me without sounding crazy.

We drank and ate chips, and I learned they were from Beacon Hill and attended college, John at Harvard and Teddy, Dartmouth. They asked me what I did.

"Well, I'm sixteen, going into my senior year of high-school."

Teddy held out his hand. "I told you. Pay up, brother."

John said, "Shoot." He took a five-dollar bill from his backpack and threw it at his brother.

John looked at me and shook his head. "Damn! You are gorgeous and don't look sixteen, your body is…sorry, I can't even say that, here want some chips?" Passing me the bag, we all laughed.

Teddy threw a small pebble at his brother's feet. "John's just looking for a wife, is all, since he turned twenty-two last month. Isn't that right, Johnny?"

Taking a pack of Marlboro's from his knapsack, John grinned. "Not exactly." He lit one and I inhaled since I loved the smell of a freshly lit cigarette. Cigarettes and beer went good together and I wanted one, but I didn't want a neighbor to see me and give me a lecture.

With my towel across my lap I took a handful of chips and placed them in a row. The warm sun had dried me and the mixture of chips, sun and beer was delightful. "I'm going to Provincetown with a guy who I'm seeing, he's in his twenties, is that bad? I mean, it's not illegal or anything, is it?"

John nodded to his brother. "He's the one studying law, what do you say, counselor?"

Teddy took a handful of chips. "Massachusetts legal age of sexual consent is sixteen. John won't date a teenager, though, he's got standards."

John said, "Damn right."

"I don't think Quinn knows I'm sixteen since I met him at a club." Teddy offered me the chip bag again. He had the same tattoo as John, although his was on his arm, black writing in a red heart.

"You guys both have that date, is it okay if I ask what it means?"

"You just did." John laughed and got three more beers.

I felt myself turn red. They both had smart humor, and I didn't have that much experience with it since most of my guy friends were usually stoned.

Teddy said, "It's in honor of our brother Patrick, who was killed in Vietnam."

That made me so sad my eyes filled. "Wow, I'm so sorry you guys." Tears were rolling down my cheeks, I didn't understand why I was so upset and felt embarrassed. I wiped my face on my arm and pulled my hair back, letting the sun soak my tears.

John took a long drag of his cigarette. "You're a sweetie pie, aren't you?"

Again, I didn't know how to answer that, yes I was a sweetie pie, no I was kind of messed up? I didn't know if I should tell them about the anti-war activity my family was involved with and decided it wasn't a good idea.

With my eyes closed and face warm, I felt so relaxed. There was a shadow and a movement, and when I opened my eyes, Mom stood over me in her black one piece, her straw hat crooked on her head.

"Mom."

She was unsteady and I realized she had been drinking all afternoon at her card game.

"I saw you from my chair with these two handsome men," she said, her British accent slurring. She threw her head back and eyed Teddy and John in a way that made me hate her.

"John, Teddy, meet my mom."

"Hi Mom," John said as he stood and shook her hand. Teddy did the same.

"Call me Sylvie, please. I'm more your age than my daughter."

John and Teddy exchanged some kind of look. I was so embarrassed and wanted her gone.

"I love the name John. Do you have a spare ciggie-poo?" John handed her a cigarette and lit it for her. She grabbed onto his arm for balance, smiling.

Mom. You are so obvious, please, walk away, you spoil everything good. She just stood there as John and Teddy sat back down.

"Mom, can I stay in Provincetown this weekend with friends?" The question seemed to confuse her, made her get back to a parent role, and she looked at me as if I was a stranger.

"Yes, lovey, of course." She glanced back at her friends. "Better get back, card game awaits." She leaned over towards my cheek for a kiss and I jumped up, lest she fall flat on her face. I took her arm and walked her most of the way. Barry met us half-way, his arm extended and smiling with his fake white teeth. Mom turned with a wave and I watched as Barry helped her into the chair.

When I got back, Rolling Stones were playing and I braced myself for remarks which thankfully never came. We sat and listened as John blew smoke rings, Teddy closed his eyes and we all sang along; the song was about violence, war, love. I was thinking about their brother Patrick and wondered if they were too. I hoped they weren't thinking about my mom. When the song ended, John drained his beer and stood up.

"Swim?"

We walked down to the water as people gazed at us, and I pictured we were gorgeous and model-looking. We stopped waist deep and watched a high wave before us.

"This one!" I yelled and we all jumped under the wave.

We swam and rode waves. When we were floating over gentle curls, John splashed me and grinned. "You're smart to ask your mom for permission in front of friends and after cocktails. My brothers and I would wait until martini hour for our requests."

Treading water, Teddy laughed. "Yeah, most often it was successful, except to borrow their cars. They never wanted us to drive them, so when we were eighteen they bought us our own."

"Are you twins?"

John said, "Teddy's the baby, he's twenty."

"I'm the baby too," I said. "Not of seven though, of two."

John smiled and nodded, his head bobbing with the waves that were becoming choppy. That's all that was said about Mom. We swam as the hot sun beat down, we body surfed until the afternoon faded, we were soaked beach bums as we made our way to the blanket, throwing ourselves down, sun drenched, salt filled, happy.

After a while, John said, "We need to hit the road, I'm driving Teddy back to Dartmouth."

I felt the pout coming and forced myself to smile, ending up with a lopsided grin. I didn't want them to leave. As I helped them pack up, John wrote on a napkin. "Here's my number, I live in Harvard Square. If you ever need anything, whatever, a ride, place to crash, rescuing, you call me. Okay?"

His blue eyes were sincere and I had a lump in my throat, tears threatening—it was as if he knew about last weekend or something. Saying goodbye was sad, but I was happy about meeting these brothers, and happier still that this weekend I was going to Provincetown with Quinn and his band.

After they left, I rode my bike to the Penny Candy store. Every summer I went many times and hadn't gone once this summer. It was a store in a small house on Nantasket Ave, inside were shelves and shelves of big glass jars filled with every kind of candy, all for a penny except a few items that were five cents. The door was low, so I ducked my head and grabbed a brown paper bag, filling it with wax lips, white chocolate pieces, strips of candy buttons, peanut butter cups, red-hots, bazooka bubble gum, Bonomos Turkish taffy, Mary Janes, mint juleps, smarties and a candy necklace which I put on. The cash register lady was new from last summer, a thin woman, her hair up in a net, with a lot of blue eye shadow, who counted my purchases in a disinterested way. If I worked here I would get so fat and develop illnesses.

My purchase was $1.50 so I had to put a few things back but still left with a huge bag of candy. Riding home, I planned what clothes to pack for my weekend with Quinn. If I had a chance to play piano this weekend I hoped it would sound good. It had been awhile since I practiced. After I put my bike Aragorn in the shed, I skipped into the house to go pack. Everything was coming together. Farmhouse guy would soon disappear from my thoughts.

CHAPTER FOURTEEN: PROVINCETOWN

When Friday came around I woke up early, excited to start my weekend. I had already packed and needed to leave Mom the note:

MOM REMINDER, going to P-town, back on Sunday. Love, Jez.

I drew a heart and left it by the tea kettle since she went there right after she woke up. In my room, I grabbed my duffle bag, stuck some of my magic stones in my pocket, got my penny candy bag and waited on the front steps. Quinn had said 9:30, so I watched people riding by on their bikes and walking. I counted cars, trying to guess which one was his. An old light blue van drove by, did a U-turn and stopped at the curb. Quinn opened the van door and stood on our sidewalk.

He was here, real and smiling, right in front of me. He wore loose linen shorts, a black tee-shirt with his hair in a neat ponytail. I ran and gave him a huge hug.

"My sweetie pie Jezzy," Quinn said, kissing me softly on the lips.

I threw my duffle bag in the back which was filled with instruments, wires, speakers and suitcases and hopped in the passenger seat with my bag of candy. "Yay, road trip," I said, as we drove off.

The windows were open blowing warm air and there was one long seat so I scooted over. Quinn put his arm around me, his smell of spice making me feel giddy. Soon we were buzzing along the highway, and I opened a pack of smarties, handing Quinn some. He pulled me close and gave me a kiss that tasted so good, better than candy. My body tingled and he grew through his baggy shorts.

"I'd pull over if we didn't have a rehearsal soon," he said, looking down at himself.

"Where, here?" We were on a road with sandy shoulders and not that many trees.

"Anywhere. Everywhere."

It was so good being with him and he was so handsome, his soft green eyes drifting from the road to me and back, and I traced his smooth face with my fingertip, wanting to know everything about him. "Where did you grow up?"

"Vermont," Quinn said. "My folks are from Boston and they moved to Vermont right before I was born, since they wanted a vegetable farm. Dad got a teaching job at a college. It was a cool place to grow up."

When he said Vermont, it reminded me of that night the whole family was together last month, the end of June. The family dinner with the fight when I watched those hippies walk down the alley. That night I had envisioned running away with the hippies to their Vermont cabin, and here Quinn was telling me he was from Vermont. It was all so mystical. I touched the stones in my pocket as I listened to him talk about his family. They sounded so nice and normal.

We rolled into Provincetown behind a line of cars, and drove past art galleries with their doors open and paintings on the sidewalk. Tourists, gay guys in their next to nothing bathing suits, lesbians holding hands, smells of fish and cotton candy, all sights I loved from my past visits greeted us. We parked by a club on Commercial Street and I helped Quinn unload the van. It was hot and humid again. I wondered if there was time for us to jump in the ocean before his rehearsal.

The steps into the club were rickety and inside, big fans blew warm air. His band sat around the bar looking sweaty, drinking bottles of beer. A baby grand piano sat in the corner where guys were setting up microphones and a big, tall woman with thick muscles stood behind the bar watching everything. She had pale white skin, wore a lavender baseball hat, suspenders, a lavender sleeveless tee and jean shorts to her knees with bulky muscles bulging. She must stay in the club all the time since she was so pale. Why not visit the beach, I wondered?

"That's the owner," Quinn whispered. Another woman was behind the bar with a rag wiping the counter. She was skinny, pretty, with wavy, blond hair, tan skin and wore a pretty, flowered dress. I felt nervous that Quinn would get a crush on her. He didn't seem to notice her though as he joined the band on stage. Unsure of my role, I wandered over to the baby grand and sat, playing a few chords, the keys soft and smooth.

The assistant woman was passing around sandwiches and came over with her tray. She had orange-red lipstick on a full mouth, and a flowery smell.

"You're the piano player?" She handed me a sandwich.

"I wish, I'm just learning." The sandwich was tasty and different, cheese and some green mushy stuff. "Yum, what is this?"

She laughed. "Cheese and avocado."

"I never had this, it's great."

After she left with her tray, Quinn came over, put his arm around me, and said they were going to rehearse. I wished I was good enough to play something, surprise all the other musicians. They'd ask me if I would play a song tonight. Humbly, I would nod.

"Jez, you can stay or take a bike through town, go to the beach, whatever you want. They're letting us stay here, upstairs, which is great." He ran his finger down my arm.

As a serious musician, I should stay, yet the room was stuffy and hot. Quinn noticed my hesitation.

"Go swimming, Jez, this will be boring, and later today Shannon will show you some stuff on the piano."

"Really?"

"Sure."

The bikes were at the side of the house. They were all rusty but the tires were good, so I picked one with a basket in front. My bathing suit was under my clothes, and I grabbed my beach bag and towel, sweat dripping from my arms, a mosquito buzzing around my head. It landed on my wrist and I flicked it away, a spot of blood appearing. Quinn kissed me and I rode off through town, dodging pedestrians, other bikes and cars.

By the time I reached the beach it was so hot I didn't bother walking to the nude part, just parked my bike, ran over hot sand, threw off my clothes and jumped into the surf. This sand was coarser than my beach and the sea was much warmer, waves big and choppy. Diving under a white cap my body cooled. In and out of waves, floating, everything felt wrong, even the ocean as it chopped around me. An undertow pulled and thick clouds appeared overhead.

I body surfed to the shore and pulled my towel around my shoulders, wishing I stayed at the club. This was my big chance—this Provincetown trip—why did I go alone to the beach, which I do every day, instead of staying at rehearsal? A real musician would have stayed. Feeling stupid, I raced back through town, almost ramming into a bunch of guys crossing the street.

At the club, I leaned the bike near the garbage cans, flies buzzing, rotten smells thick with heat. The meditation book talked about an Indian saint named Zipruanna who meditated on piles of waste, uplifted and unbothered. Queen Jezebel would know her next right step. From now on I would pretend I was her.

The screen door shuddered from a big piece of blue tape unsuccessfully closing a huge rip. Inside, the lead singer was in the middle of a song, with the band playing. I leaned against a wooden beam and listened, the music helping me connect again to my purpose. This was where I was supposed to be. When the song was finished,

Quinn came over.

"How was the beach? Come on, let's see our room." There was a door near the bar that he opened and then we climbed steep steps to the second floor. Our room was number three, and after we walked in Quinn closed the door quickly and grabbed me. He kissed me deeply, pressing his hard penis against my body, making me squirm.

"You taste salty and so sweet," he said, as he took off my clothes and bikini, leading me to the bed. There was an off-white, bumpy bedspread which felt weird on my skin.

"Hang on." I peeled off the spread and threw it in the corner. The room was tiny, with a small, dirty, plastic fan that sputtered in the corner. I lay on the sheet. "Better."

Quinn kissed my shoulders and arms which was delightful and ticklish. He took his clothes off and I ran my hands down his long, lean, smooth as silk body. We lay beside each other and I felt his chest which was dripping with sweat. I put my hand on his penis which made him moan. Fumbling over the pillows, he reached for a condom.

"Yes," I might have said, or thought; in the haze of love all I could think of was feeling him in me as close as possible. I grabbed onto his back. He moved slowly, and then fast and we were a flame, his sounds a roar that excited me, I just wanted to stay in this place forever. After he came, he kissed me so deep and there was nothing else, only this bliss.

The fan whirled and blew warm air around the tiny space.

"I'm going to do you in the shower," he said, grinning, his long hair messy as he pulled me up. There were two white fluffy towels on the chair which he grabbed, and we ran down the hall to the shared bathroom. The shower was tiny, so we were squished, laughing. He soaped me all over. Between my legs he was gentle, his fingers touched inside and out, caressing. He put the soap down and let the water rinse over me, then knelt on the shower floor, burying his face in me like I was some tasty treat. I braced my hands on the glass, knees wobbly, my whole body aroused with his thick, beautiful tongue. Soon I exploded, my body ripples and waves. My knees gave and I slid down, joining him on the slippery tiles.

Water ran over us. He held my hand, playing with my fingers. My toenails were long and dirty from bare-feet and I didn't even care. Putting my head on his shoulder, I felt secure and protected. Closing my eyes there was a flash of that other shower. I opened my eyes and stared at Quinn. Be present, I told myself. That day was a bad dream, a mistake. This is real, this is true.

The water turned cool and soon freezing which felt great for a second before Quinn jumped up and turned it off. He opened the glass door. "Come on, sweet Jezzy, time for a nap."

Wrapped in towels, we walked down the hall into our room, sliding under the clean crisp sheets. The fan clicked, blowing on our cooled bodies as we breathed together into rest.

Someone was knocking on our door yelling, "Sound check, sound check."

The side clock said 7:00, the sky beyond our window was grey, dusk.

"Oh, shit." Quinn jumped up. We dressed. Quinn wore a black linen shirt with linen shorts and sneakers, and I put on my favorite lime green sundress that showed off my tan.

"You look beautiful," he said, kissing my shoulders as we walked down the hall, down the steep steps and into the club. The owner and the flowered dress woman were behind the bar and a huge table had been set up with barbecue. Quinn went for the sound check and I didn't know if I should take any food. One of the band members was piling a plate and he noticed me looking.

He handed me a plate. "Dig in, my friend." Gratefully, I took some barbecue chicken, beans, pulled pork, corn on the cob, corn bread, collard greens. At a quiet table away from people, I sat and ate. Smoky, spicy tastes filled me. Quinn was talking with the piano player who walked over to my table. I froze, mid-bite of cornbread, wondering if I had sauce all over my face.

"Hi, Jezebel, I'm Shannon. Quinn said you play piano?"

My voice sounded muffled as I swept the napkin over my face. "Yes, I play a little and want to learn jazz, I know scales and some chords and whatnot."

I felt idiotic and childish, but she didn't seem to notice.

"Did you ever learn 7th chords, minor chords, more complex beats?"

I shook my head.

"I can show you later or tomorrow at our Cambridge gig, at Jacks. I'll introduce you to some other piano players, help you find a teacher." She turned, glancing at the food table.

"Thanks, Shannon, that sounds great, and, ah, you said Cambridge? Quinn said we were here until Sunday."

She laughed and shook her head. "He never gets the schedule right; he plays with a lot of different bands. I'll let him know what's up."

The cornbread was sweet and moist and I washed it down with pink lemonade. Cambridge tomorrow, more musicians! Jacks! Maybe Sparky would be there. Everything was unfolding perfectly. I brushed crumbs from my dress and scratched a few mosquito bites on my wrist. Quinn came to my table with a plate piled high with food, guests started to arrive, club lights were dimming, jazz was piped in and night time was settling.

At performance time, I stayed at the back table, my eyes closed, relaxed. Loud laughter came from one of the tables and I glared at five guys wearing muscle shirts doing shots and not listening. At the next table an older couple clapped after solos, as did most people. Quinn played a harmonica solo and everyone burst into applause and I was so happy he was mine. There was a group of touristy looking adults in front with logo tees, straw hats and sandals, nodding and tapping their feet.

The owner went to a table of women and brought drinks, waving away their money. She looked my way, glancing at what I was drinking which was a glass of pink lemonade. In my dress pocket was my real license, not my fake ID, and since I was with Quinn I didn't think it mattered. The owner was wearing a black vest over a sleeveless tee that said, "Womyn Unite", and I wondered if it was a feminist thing, spelling it wrong.

At the break Quinn motioned me over to the bar where Shannon and other band members had gathered.

"That was great," I said as he put his arm around me. "Hey, Shannon said it's Cambridge tomorrow, not here, did she tell you?"

He raised his eyes. "Yeah, I got it wrong again. Can you still come?"

"Yes!"

Quinn ordered us two Molson's. The owner stopped running her rag over the counter and stared at me. "I need some ID."

She went to help someone else and Quinn shook his head. "She can be tough—you have a license?"

The thought of lying, pretending I didn't have it, crossed my mind. But honesty and being true to myself, like Queen Jezebel, was the new path I was on. I took my license from my dress pocket and placed it on the bar counter.

Snatching it up, Quinn smiled. "Pretty picture, they're usually bad." He looked closer at my ID. "Ah, what?" With wide eyes, he turned, faced me, and whispered a low, dreadful note. "You're sixteen?"

Panic ran through me watching his body slump. No, Quinn, don't slump, it's still me. You can still love me. "Hey, I didn't lie about my age, I've been sixteen this whole time. You never asked me, and I'll be seventeen in October."

He stared at the bottles on the shelf. "I guess since I met you at a club…I just figured you were older…wow…"

The owner came back and Quinn said, "One Molson, one coke." She smirked, and I wanted to reach over the bar and punch her muscled huge misspelled stomach.

Quinn walked away to play his second set and I was left, interrupted and steaming, a part of me lost, with the urge to hide. At my table in back, two guys sat, kissing. A stool was open at the end of the bar so I took it, avoiding the eyes of the owner knowing she could tell me to leave if she wanted. Music played and my ears felt blocked, the only sound was my furious train of thoughts—what was going to happen, would he still love me, am I still part of this thing? What about Sparky? After half listening I walked outside, music at my back. I sat on the curb and watched flies dance beneath streetlights.

A tall lady wearing high heels who was a man walked by pushing a baby carriage with a little dog sitting wearing a sailor hat. The dog turned its head and stared at me. Applause erupted from inside and I scowled at the dog.

"Hey." Quinn sat next to me on the curb.

I stuck my fingernail into a very itchy mosquito bite, digging hard, drawing blood which made a droplet on my wrist.

"Jezzy," he said. His eyes had mirrors of sadness which I wanted to smash before they could multiply.

"No."

He took my hand. "No?"

"No, I'm not going."

He half-smiled and shook his head. "You don't have to go tonight."

The word 'tonight' hit me, and soon a cloud, fog, some laughter, a yell, and twenty errant moths were between us. I held onto a wing and hoped to fly away.

Taking a handful of my hair, Quinn softly sang, "Jezebel, too good to be true, Jezebel, it's all the blues."

Tears erupted, falling down my face, and I put my head in his lap. "I'm not a song." Stroking my hair, he hummed, wordless, soothing.

I gazed at him from his lap. "You're not so much older than me. Are you religious so you're moralistic?"

Laughing, Quinn said, "I'm twenty-two, not religious, and yes, I have morals. So do you, Jezzy."

"Yeah, my morals are I'm a nice person and I don't kill spiders. And you're only six years older than me, besides." This had to be an aberration of a perfect plan, a tear in the flawless performance, just a small bump that I rode over on my bicycle.

"You're still a high school student," he said, melancholy playing on his lips.

Sitting up, I kissed him on his soft lips. "It doesn't matter, age isn't important. I'm an old soul."

"A sweet soul." He turned as Shannon, on the porch, called him over and we went inside. The food was back on the table, and everyone was eating. Guests were mingling or leaving. The owner wasn't in sight, so I grabbed a bottle of beer and chugged half of it, glaring around.

Shannon, unaware of disquietude, took my hand and led me to the piano.

"Here, watch," she said. She showed me a few seventh chords, minor chords and a basic blues bass line with the left hand.

"You play the bass line," she said.

As we played, a guy picked up his sax and the drummer came over. Quinn got his harmonica and we started to jam. At first I was nervous, but then I relaxed and even added a few new notes as we got into the song. Everything else disappeared—my fear, my thoughts, and only the music existed. When the song ended, the sax player nodded at me and the drummer shook my hand.

Shannon gave me a hug as she got up from the piano. "You'll do great, Jezebel."

Blues played from speakers, people crowded the bar, others sat at their tables, thick with belonging, and I was alone on stage, waiting for the next song. I couldn't leave this scene. It was the best thing ever. Quinn sat next to me on the piano bench.

My bottom lip must have dropped because he looked at me with a pout and held my hand. "That sounded great, Jez."

I leaned against him. "This is the best thing that's ever happened, please don't take it away."

"Nothing is going, sweet girl, the music is inside of you."

Musicians drifted, it was late, my eyes were tired, the club was emptying and somewhere close a dog was howling. Quinn and I went up the steep stairs to our room. The windows were flung open and the bed was made, the broken fan gone. Slipping off my flip flops, I hugged the pillow and watched Quinn take off his sneakers and stare at the sky. Was he sleeping with me, was he staying? I was relieved when he lay down, and I curled around his body. We held each other and I inhaled his smell of beer, woods, spice.

Inside we drifted to sleep and outside, crickets chirped their tune, a chorus. The air stilled with its thick warmth. August, my most desperate month, the one that held me at bay, always offering me a chance to escape, had once again teased me into thinking I was found.

CHAPTER FIFTEEN: RESCUE

Musical notes swarmed my brain as I opened my eyes. Quinn wasn't there and I felt panic. Was that it, did he leave? Taking a quick shower, I thought of the last shower we took together when everything was fun and better. Maybe Quinn would change his mind and let me stay.

Back in the room I stuffed everything in my duffle bag including a starfish from the decorative items they had on the dresser. I ran down the cheap broken steps and through the flimsy screen door. Quinn's van was parked at the curb and two guys were loading speakers and instruments into the back.

"Hey, Jezzy," Quinn said, reaching for me. "We need to leave soon, Saturday traffic sucks. I can drop you at your beach house before Cambridge."

I waited until we were alone. "I'm not going home."

His inhale was ragged. "Jezebel, sweet girl…"

"I'm not your sweet girl anymore and I'm going to Cambridge. I have a lot of friends there, not just you."

I unwrapped a piece of grape bazooka, stuck it in my mouth and began reading the comic strip that was sticky from the gum, attempting to act like I didn't care and that I hadn't just lied about tons of friends in Cambridge.

A few minutes later I was in the passenger seat as we made our way through Provincetown traffic. Soon we were breezing on the highway. I didn't look at Quinn, didn't want to see his soft green eyes or remember the feel of his body, didn't want the smell of him hypnotizing me. The van windows were open, the air thick with heat.

Everything bad happened on really hot days— farm house, Quinn not loving me anymore.

He reached his arm in the backseat and retrieved a wrapped egg sandwich, giving me half. After taking a few bites, he began talking, his voice melodic with notes of caring. "Jez, this is my fault and I'm sorry. It's not that I don't want to be with you, God, I love being with you. If you were just a few years older—you have to understand, I can't even bring you to Jack's tonight. We could lose our job and Jack's is a great gig for us, they have big names and playing there as the main act is a huge deal."

The egg tasted dry and I put my sandwich down. "I've already been there, and Shannon said she'd introduce me around. Sparky might be there. I have to go, Quinn, it's my path."

He reached for my hand. I wanted to explain about everything that led up to now. Queen Jezebel, inner courage, meditation, being a musician, seeing him in the alley that night, meeting him at Jack's, Sparky, all of it fitting together. But I didn't have the words to describe the picture in my head.

From my candy bag, I extracted two long paper strips of candy buttons, handing one to Quinn. It was so hard being angry; he was so kind which made it all wrong. For the next few minutes there was silence as we bit the little colorful candy buttons off the paper. Half way through, I tossed mine back in the bag. "These aren't worth all the work."

He laughed. "I know what you mean, kind of like lobster."

"Quinn, please just forget my age and be with me anyway, okay?"

His answer was a sigh and taking my hand. There was a cassette player in his car and I put in a Grateful Dead tape, which made me think about Grey and all my Newton friends. Who I missed. And now I would miss Quinn, too. It was so unfair.

I must have dozed because when my eyes opened Harvard Square loomed before us. Brattle Street was crowded with Saturday shoppers, and Quinn pulled the van over in front of a record store. Music blasted from a huge speaker on the sidewalk, a song that used to make me laugh about someone going fishing, a real silly song. It wasn't funny today, though.

I shook off my sleepiness, grabbed my bag and avoided Quinn's eyes. The city was thick and dusty. We leaned against his van. I didn't want to leave him but wasn't about to beg. He put his arms around me, held me close, and I dropped my bag and buried my head in his cotton tee-shirt, breathing in his smell. He cupped my face and kissed me soft on my lips, and I put my hands in his back pockets, not wanting to let go. Quinn started humming in my ear and we floated together, a crest. Our breath was one and he whispered, "Jezebel."

I wouldn't be the one to hang on longest, like a toddler holding onto a parents' leg. Letting go of him, tears spilled down my cheeks. I let my hair fall over my face as I turned away, the hot city pavement burning some strange divide, moving me away into the pulse of some unknown wandering.

The little church yard with old gravestones appeared dark even though the sun was shining. My duffle bag was heavy and I had a weird impulse to lie between the gravestones and feel cool dirt on my face to dissolve this glut of feelings. I'd meditate amongst the dead and peace would overcome me. My tenth-grade art class had come here, an all-day trip for gravestone rubbings which ended with eating at Bartley's burgers, the rolled-up charcoal rubbings underneath our arms.

I crossed to Cambridge Common and plopped on a bench. People were setting up for a Saturday evening concert, Hare Krishnas chanted across the green by a fountain, their bells ringing, and a sitar twanged a hollow haunted sound. The Krishnas were serving food to street people from a big, white van.

I'm a street person now. I have no food and don't know where I'm sleeping tonight. Hobos stood in line with their wagons and shopping carts full of their belongings.

There was a roar of engines and smell of grease emanating from the street where motorcycles were idling. I closed my eyes, hoping for direction. Do I take the ferry and call Mom from Pemberton Point or Hingham? Then I would be defeated, my weekend a failure, everything unfinished.

Loud yelling and laughter interrupted my ruminating, as groups of biker guys and girls entered the Common with blankets, coolers, bags, all wearing leather vests with emblems of their gangs which I couldn't read, yet seemed similarly ominous. Rock and roll music blasted from a speaker as they set up their blankets in front of the stage and around the green. Time for me to move. Yet I was frozen.

A guy came over, one of the bikers. He had faded black tattoos up and down his thick arms, a red bandana on his head with a dark mustache and beard. "Hey, you look lonely, come join us, we have plenty of food and beer." He smiled and had straight teeth that were surprisingly bright white.

I sat up straight and put my hand on my bag. "I have to meet a friend, thanks anyway." Someone had started a bonfire which smelled woodsy, there was a barbecue giving off tempting steak odors and I was hungry. He must have seen the pause in me and took a few steps closer. "Just for a little while until your friend gets here," he said as he eyed my duffle bag.

My breath caught. I looked like a runaway, anybody's girl, or no one's. A bunch of firecrackers went off and I jumped. He reached his hand towards me.

Think quick, Jezebel.

"Everything is the Self," I stated, standing quickly, forcing a lopsided grin that along with my words must have seemed crazy, because he dropped his hand and stepped away, his expression confused. Grabbing my bag, I held my head high, marched away and focused on the street, Hare Krishna bells in one ear and rock and roll, the other.

Walking straight with my eyes focused and breathing steadily made me feel calmer, and I found myself beside the gates of Harvard University. Students hurried, carrying books, even on the edge of a Saturday night. Their purposeful movements inspired me and I knew my next step was to find a place to stay. At a payphone, I stuck in two dimes, called Amy and listened to it ring about twenty times before I remembered she was back in Maine. No one picked up at Eric's, my sister was at Jacob's Pillow. The thought of Rachel made me sad—my summer had become a mess without her. She was a bus ride away, I could stay with her, except, she was dancing, busy with her life. Calling Dad was not an option—after our last interaction at fried clams lunch with Bubbie, there was no way.

Feeling tired and angry at Quinn who was down the road playing at Jack's, I leaned against the door of the phone booth wondering how it would be if I showed up at Jack's. It wasn't fair, I missed him and yearned for that whole music scene with hip musicians, casual conversations, the feeling of belonging.

Someone tapped on the door. A young Asian woman with dark hair, wearing a Harvard tee-shirt, smiled. "Sorry? I need to phone someone?"

"No, I'm sorry, here."

I stepped onto the sidewalk feeling dumb. Here I was in Harvard land with nowhere to go, no brains in my head, just some stupid ideas, a story I had weaved creating a complex spider's web that had trapped me.

Thirst overtook me, and I opened my duffle to see if I had any money left. My small beach bag was there and I shook its contents on top of my duffle. Shells, a piece of sea glass, crumbs, a squished-up

napkin and a five-dollar bill emerged covered with sand. I brushed the
sand away, stuck the money in my pocket and was about to throw the
napkin away when I spotted written: JOHN SHEEHAN 617-876-
6831.

It was John from the beach and he said call anytime I needed and
here it was, two days later, and I needed. I stared at the number, then
across the street at the strong, confident buildings of Harvard. They
infused me with a kind of resolve previously lost, so I went into the
now empty phone booth and inserted my coins.

"John here."

He answered so quickly that my voice disappeared.

"Hello?"

"Hey, John, it's Jezebel from the beach? We met…"

"Jezebel from the beach, of course I know who you are, nice to hear
from you."

I told him I was stuck and without asking any questions, he said
come over. As I walked to his building, my steps slowed as butterflies
of hesitation danced on my bones. My decisions lately were so wrong
and I didn't trust myself. Was this smart and courageous or another
dumb move. The farmhouse man, messing things up with Quinn, lying
about having a place to stay tonight.

John and Teddy seemed nice at the beach. Still, this was me going
to his apartment. Was I piling up bad choices? Did I need to be more
selective, like when I picked up seashells on the beach and tossed away
cracked ones?

His building was a brick townhouse and looked innocent enough,
and as I stood in front gazing at the windows, I took a small stone
from my pocket and pressed its cool, smooth surface to my cheek. The
sky turned dark, days were shorter on the crest of that hazy, sad end
of summer. Leaning against a tree I watched a laughing Indian couple
get buzzed into his building as a group of students walked out. An

unusually tall man exited being pulled by a tiny dog that I thought was a cat. It sniffed at me and the man pulled it away, hurrying down the sidewalk. Laughter came from an open window with the smell of weed. My mouth was so dry. Ring John's bell, or find another way? Come on magic stone, give me direction.

The door opened again and John stepped onto the sidewalk, wearing a white tee, jeans and flip-flops. He glanced around and spotted me, and to my relief his face lit up and his dimples smiled.

Walking over, he glanced at my duffle bag. "Hey, Jezebel, I thought you might have gotten lost."

Even though we had just met this week, John felt familiar, comfortable. "Hi, no, not lost…just…thanks for coming down."

Two young women left his building, both with long hair wearing short-shorts, one Black and the other white, both beautiful.

"Hi John," they said almost at the same time, and giggled.

"Ladies," he said as he tipped a pretend cap. Was I interrupting his Saturday night, being a pest?

"Hey, are you busy, I mean, it's Saturday and all…"

He shook his head. "It's early, don't worry about me. Want to come up or grab food?"

He was so happy and clean and still I worried, my judgment was like that broken fan last night, wobbly and then gone. John looked at me for a longish glance, picked up my duffle and led me to the corner where there was a small restaurant with lowlights and just a few patrons.

"They don't serve alcohol here so weekends are pretty quiet." The waitress put tall glasses of water on the table and I drank mine in three gulps, then excused myself, needing to pee. When I got back, we ordered burgers and iced tea. Classical music played beneath a low murmur of eaters.

"So what happened with your Provincetown weekend?"

"You remembered."

"Of course." His hair was wet and his face was shaved and smooth. I felt awkward and inarticulate, way different than last night when I played with the band and had a cool boyfriend.

"Well…P-town was fun at first. We were at a club, I got to jam with the band and I learned some new stuff on the piano. Everything was going great until Quinn, my boyfriend, learned I was only sixteen. He thought that since we met at Jack's I was older. But I didn't lie to him, John, it just never came up. Quinn said he couldn't be with a high schooler, it wasn't right. So, he broke up with me."

The burgers came and I took a few bites before I continued. "They have a gig in Cambridge tonight and he was going to drop me home but I said no way. See, my weekend wasn't over and I was supposed to find a piano teacher Sparky, so I wasn't going home without that. I told him I had friends to stay with, otherwise he wouldn't have dropped me off, he's a good guy. That was my only lie, I was mad because I love him…"

Those stupid tears rolled down my face and I ducked my head.

John reached across the table and took my hand. "He's a decent guy, Jez, and didn't want to mess with your head. I mean, you have so much going for you."

"I do?"

"Sure, you're smart, beautiful, creative, energetic …"

It was as if he was talking about someone else. "Really?"

"That's what I see."

"Except, my choices have been bad lately. It's like I'm missing something inside me."

John shook his head. "You're not missing anything, Jezebel. Sounds like you have a rough situation with your parents." He had a funny expression on his face and then I remembered he met Mom, she flirted with him on the beach. Ugh.

"Yeah, well, I learned to meditate and that's been helpful. Also I'm looking for a jazz piano teacher, I thought that would help me escape my parents—Mom has a boyfriend this summer, even though she's still married to my Dad, and my Dad, well …"

My face burned and I wished I could stop talking. A switch had been turned on and I didn't know what I might say. Dad had started acting weird again, last weekend in Amherst I was almost raped and killed. I hadn't told anyone about the farm house and it was still locked inside me like some disease, festering. But I didn't want that to leak out, so I shook my head to shut off the faucet of words.

John said, "You're a truth seeker. That's cool, but it makes it hard to pretend, you can't turn away from things, especially if they feel wrong."

"Yes, you get it!"

A group of students came in and one guy nodded at John. Lights dimmed, and the music turned jazzy.

"It's great you started meditation, Jezebel. Last year one of my philosophy professors taught meditation and it really helped with clarity, balance, everything." He got the check and I handed him my five.

"You keep that, my treat," he said, glancing at his watch. "How about I drive you home?"

"What about your night? I don't want to ruin it."

"Jez, don't worry, it's all good."

Leaving the restaurant, I followed him like a puppy. "Wow, thanks so much, I didn't know what I was going to do or anything. Really, that's so nice."

We walked to where his car was parked on a quiet side street, a black BMW that suited him. I wanted to be older and marry him, live in Cambridge with all the musicians and smart minds, let everything influence me and become an intelligent, talented person.

We drove down Mass Ave. and were soon buzzing on the highway with windows open and the radio playing.

"This is Fats and that was Herbie Hancock, you can see Herbie Hancock live all this week at the Jazz Workshop. You're listening to WBCN, and we're in Boston. Coming up at midnight, young enough to dance and sing old enough to get that swing, Little Bill will be here with another night of Teenage Madness."

Pointing at the radio, I said, "Little Bill, I know him! We were in ninth grade together, he's famous now and that's his radio show. He knows all the jazz people and he's my age." From the radio came the tinkle of piano keys. "I wish we were still friends and he could help me find Sparky, the piano teacher I'm looking for."

A slow, melodic saxophone played. I hunched down in the comfortable leather seats as we drove by Boston Harbor with lights from boats, piers and the highway all blending together against a dark, black background.

"You'll get a teacher, Jezebel, I'm confident of that. Don't give up."

"Will you and Teddy be at the beach again?"

"One of my courses starts this week, but maybe, with my books."

"Cool, what course?"

"Nietzsche."

"Wow, I heard of him."

John laughed and told me about his Ph.D. program in moral and political philosophy which sounded fascinating, about thought, morals, religion. Even though I didn't understand all of what he said it resonated within me, reminding me of my connection with the ocean and all its octopus' arms of shells, sea glass, sand and salt.

We breezed along and soon the familiar sight of the Hingham boat yard appeared, with air turning cooler. The smell of low tide, crabs, fish, the tanginess of salt, welcomed me back home. John pulled up in front of my house.

"Thank you so much." I hugged him and he took my hand as we faced each other, his expression almost smiling yet serious.

"Jezebel. Think. Be safe. Take pause. And, you have my number."

He sped off down the road. His wisdom, kindness, and generosity overwhelmed me.

The house was quiet. Mom's door was closed, and I entered my bedroom, dropped the duffle and walked to the bathroom. I let hot water run over my itchy mosquito bites. In the mirror was my same face, same brown eyes, tan skin, thick eyebrows, brown hair, and something else, unnamed. John's words had changed me, and a new feeling pulsed inside. Quiet yet insistent.

CHAPTER SIXTEEN: POPSICLE STICKS

Kipper smell woke me. Kippers: a strong, salty fish that Mom made when happy. Through the curtains showed a grey, cloudy Sunday. Amidst kipper smells were that of bacon and toast, so I threw on my sweatshirt and headed down the hall. I heard Mom's cheery voice and a man's laughter, not Dad's.

I peed and brushed my teeth, then opened the door a crack to the clatter of plates. A man was setting dishes on the table, his back to me. Barry—did he stay here last night? Was it because Mom thought I was in Provincetown and I wasn't supposed to be back until this afternoon?

Mom appeared with a steaming plate of kippers and another plate with crisp bacon, wearing light brown shorts and a yellow blouse, her face made up and hair done. When she noticed me, she abruptly stood still. "Jez, you're here." Then she recovered and smiled as if nothing unordinary was going on. "Come have breakfast." She set down the plates and went back in the kitchen.

Barry turned with a grin, his fake white teeth sparkling at me, his brown, wavy hair combed away from his overly tan, thick face. "How's your summer going?" His voice was sing-song and trying for cool. As best as I could I glared at him while bee-lining for the bacon. I stuffed two pieces in my mouth, all the while thinking, why the fuck are you in my house.

As if reading my mind, Mom left the kitchen holding a teapot. "Barry just came over for breakfast. We'll be playing cards on Mike's porch this afternoon." She kissed my cheek and went to pour tea.

"Dad's coming today, right?" I knew he wasn't and she knew I knew. Mom's eyes darted from Barry to me, her mood dulled for a moment.

"Soon."

The look Mom gave me said more than any words could: please don't stir things up, please let me have this.

"I'm leaving." I grabbed a piece of toast as Mom started to say something then stopped. In my room, stuff was on the floor amidst an ever-increasing sand pile, a damp towel crusting in the corner. A clam shell had fallen on the floor and had cracked. I held one of the heavier rocks and smashed the clam shell, watched as it fragmented into little pieces, then felt bad knowing it wasn't the shell's fault. Scooping up the fragments into my beach pail, I considered climbing onto our bike shed from my window to avoid Mom and Barry, yet it was too much trouble for idiotic people. The domestic scene of them eating breakfast together, which hadn't occurred between my parents in years, made my stomach curl. As I whisked by them Mom looked up, smiling vaguely as I left.

I hated them, was furious at Mom, and wanted to kick Barry repeatedly.

The smashed shell glistened at the bottom of my pail, and walking to the edge of the water, I tipped out the pieces, returning them to the ocean. Sorry I smashed you, shell, may you become a better shell, a conch, perhaps, or a clam with a pearl.

John said, *take pause*. My desire for destruction felt enormous as I sat by the edge of the water, hoping the coolness of the ocean would take away the too big feelings. Sun blazed through a humid mid-August day and people started piling down the beach path, as if they had been standing ready at their doors for the moment clouds cleared. My toenails were long and disgusting, staring at me as I stretched my legs, and I realized they hadn't been cut since, well, who knows when.

Take pause, cut your nails, be happy.

As I watched everyone coming down the beach a short, round tanned lady held a beach chair with difficulty. She had an insulated beach bag on her shoulder that kept slipping down her arm and finally fell on the sand. She bent to retrieve it and I recognized her, my neighbor Edith, the nice and nosy one who always invited me for baked goods. I ran over and took her chair and beach bag.

"Here, I'll help you." In her beach bag were Wise potato chips, some pink beverage in a plastic bottle with ice cubes, a plastic container full of strawberries, plaid cloth napkins and a Time magazine.

"Put my chair at our spot, my kids and grandkids will be here any minute, twelve of us today, can you believe it?"

That's right, I remembered, she had a huge family that gathered together every weekend; they sat in one of those enviable circles with husbands, kids, grandkids, food, toys, a cigar or two, and plenty of laughter. I set up her chair, putting the towel on the back. "Okay, see you."

Edith sat and reached for her strawberries. "Jezebel, sit, have a strawberry." She put the towel on the sand but I kept standing. "How's your father? I haven't seen much of him this summer." She had concern behind her eyes or was it pity? Had she seen Barry at my house?

The strawberries were bright red, perfectly shaped with green stems. "He has real estate deals this summer and travels a lot, you know, work stuff." Looking away, I hoped she'd stop talking, and thought that maybe if I took one of her strawberries she'd be satisfied, so I took the biggest one and bit into the juicy, sweet fruit.

"What about Rachel? You're all by yourself every day."

Was she criticizing or being kind? It was hard to read her expression. "Rachel has a dance scholarship and I'm getting one soon for jazz piano." This wasn't exactly a story; some elements were true.

As Edith bit into a strawberry, juice dripped down her chin. "You

Berke girls were always creative and smart, must be your genes. Your mom still paints, yes?"

I nodded. Mom had brought her easel even though she hadn't painted yet this summer.

From the dunes, Edith's family waved, and I took my leave. I had expected some negative comment about Mom and was surprised she viewed me and Rachel as creative and smart. Edith wasn't part of Mom's card circle—if she thought Mom was with Barry it would be all over town.

A white rock glittered with water and I bent to examine its patterns.

This must be what John meant. Taking pause, not reacting. It didn't feel comfortable, though, there was a trapped quality. It would be good to discuss more of his philosophical ideas next time I was in Cambridge, when I didn't need to be rescued. Just casual.

Time to claim my house back, since I needed my bathing suit and beach bag. When I reached the front door the house seemed quiet. Inside, everything was sparkling clean, dishes and food put away. Mom called me as I was getting a powdered donut and I looked down the hall where she stood, wearing her black two-piece, nice white sandals and a sunhat, holding a striped cover-up.

"Tell me what you think of this, does it make me look too full in the hips?"

She slipped the cover-up over her head as I licked the powder off my donut.

"It looks fine, Mom."

She put her hat back on. "Tonight a few friends will be over for drinks after the beach. I can't believe summer's almost over, it's been such a nice time, hasn't it?"

I couldn't look at her, never mind answer. How could I make her understand if she could ask me that? This summer I must have been a shadow to her, a lamp on the side table.

"Dad won't be here anymore, right?"

She went back to her room and I followed. "Jezebel, he hates the beach. Why even ask?" She got a beach bag and applied red lipstick. "And tonight, can you stay at a friend's house? It's not a kid's party."

"What friends, Mom? All of them are somewhere else. Haven't you even noticed?"

Barry's white Mercedes was waiting at the curb. "Well, Jez, just stay in your room or go to Paragon Park, I'm sure you'll see people you know there." Mom smoothed down her shorts.

I stuffed the donut in my mouth and followed her to the porch. To the left a group of teenagers walked to the beach with boogie boards. I felt so mad at my mom. I wanted to hurt her, ruin this thing she was having with this fake Romeo, and at the same time, she seemed so frail in her hat.

She sucked in her cheeks and walked towards his car.

"Wait, Mom!"

She turned.

"Since my friends are back in Newton, I might stay with one of them for a few days, take the ferry to Boston."

A worried look crossed her face. "Is the ferry safe?"

I stifled a laugh. Of all things, she was concerned about the ferry?

"Yes, Mom, it's safe."

She got into Barry's car as he leaned over and waved to me. I didn't wave back. Mom closed the door and they took off.

Two bees played tag in the air.

There was no way I would stay here tonight. Did Rachel know this part of Mom? What if when I told her Rachel said that I was making something of nothing, same as when I told her about Dad? She had to witness what happened this summer to believe it, and for the millionth time, I wished she was here.

In my bikini and tee-shirt, walking back to the beach, another escape plan started forming. Since Quinn was gone I had to find new musicians to hang with, ones that might know Sparky. Those Amherst musicians said they'd be in Cambridge and I wondered what date they were playing. I didn't even know what date it was today.

I rushed back to my house.

In my room their flyer was crunched up on the dresser.

LAURA & TODD PLAY JAZZ TUNES FROM THE 50's, the flyer said. It listed a bunch of other bands and at the bottom, it said, Cambridge Common Sunday Series, August 18, 1974. 8:00.

I had to figure out what today's date was. I raced to the kitchen to find Mom's appointment book. Losing track of the days was a benefit to staying at the beach all summer except now I felt stupid. There weren't any hints to where we were in August, no appointments to recognize, and last week I spent in bed- I was all mixed up.

A newspaper could tell me. We had none around the house so I hopped on my bike and rode the four blocks to Nantasket Pharmacy. While I leaned my bike against the meter I heard someone call my name. Kate was walking up to me.

"Hey, Kate, you're back from Ann Arbor!" We hugged and I stepped back, grateful to see a friend. She had cut her hair short and her face was pale instead of the usual tan, otherwise she looked the same, tall and thin with freckles and a big smile.

"How's college?"

"It's great, I'm working at a feminist bookstore and doing a lot of painting. How about you?"

In summer's past, when we were younger, Kate would instruct me, Rachel, and Carla on summer art projects. We painted shells, built boxes out of popsicle sticks that we collected on the beach, and made rope bracelets. We'd set-up a stand in front of her house and sell our wares to get enough money for penny candy.

"None of our gang's around. I'm still collecting shells and stuff, remember our stand?"

As we stood talking about her life in Michigan, I felt uncomfortable inside, because here she was talking about exhibitions, visiting artists, museums, and my life was about collecting shells and going to the pharmacy to find out the date.

"I played piano with a band in Provincetown, just for a night." It sounded so big and false.

"That's fantastic, Jez. I bet you were great. I could really see you as a performer. Tell me next time you have a gig and maybe I can come listen."

Her face was flushed and happy, she was so positive I wanted to glom onto her energy and also run away from her. I wondered what she would say, what advice she'd offer if I told her what was really going on.

"Hey, what exactly is a feminist bookstore?"

"Well, you know about the women's movement?" Kate tilted her head, curious.

"Equal pay, stop violence against women, stand up to sexist men? Like that?"

"That's part of it," she said. "We have books about feminism, novels with strong women characters, readings by women authors."

"Maya Angelou! Gloria Steinem!"

Kate laughed and nodded.

"I want to be a feminist," I said. "What do I have to do?"

"I bet you are already, Jezebel. If you want to get active, there's some places in Cambridge I can tell you about. We also organize marches, have lesbian support groups for women coming out, discussion groups about empowerment."

Her short haircut, her confidence, a new freedom about her. "Are you coming out as a lesbian?"

Kate smiled. "Jezebel, I think I've always been a lesbian, but now I can be open about it."

I nodded my head. I could see it. "Does your mom know?"

"Yeah, my parents were cool. I'm so lucky, there's women whose parents disowned them."

Wow. At this point being disowned by my parents sounded wonderful. I also wondered what it took to be a lesbian, but wasn't going to ask her that. Was I a lesbian because kissing that woman felt nice? I wasn't going to ask Kate that, either. But boy, she sure seemed happy. "Will you be at the beach later?"

Kate held up her bags which contained garden tools. "First helping Mom with the garden, beach later."

We hugged and I went into the pharmacy. The newspapers were in the back and I walked past suntan oil, towels, boogie boards, and picked up The Boston Globe. The date said Sunday, August 18.

This was kismet! Laura and Todd played tonight on Cambridge Common and Mom's party was tonight. I had a place to go and might get Laura as my piano teacher.

But where would I stay?

Riding my bike back, John's words flashed on the screen of my brain. Take pause, Jezebel. Be careful. I didn't want to make a wrong move. I really wanted to listen to his advice, and do better. No more weird guys, only positive, good people.

Back at the beach I dove underneath the crest of a wave, another wave right behind, the sun strong overhead. Many people were swimming and happy voices echoed off the surf. The three boogie board girls waved at me—the sea-glass girls, today all wearing striped bathing suits. Seagulls cried overhead.

Floating over the waves, I weighed my options.

Stay here at the beach until Mom's party was over, sneak under my own sheets and sleep in my bed, forget about Cambridge? Go to Paragon Park, play skee-ball and meet cute guys? Hitch a ride and see where I land? Go to Edith's house, eat too many cookies, fall asleep on her couch? Find Quinn and beg him to take me back? Write another letter for advice to—someone? Bubbie? The Dalai Lama?

Back on my beach towel, a seagull stood close.

"I don't have any food, seagull."

He stared at my bag as if doubting me.

"Really, I'm not lying. Let me ask your opinion. Do I stay here tonight with crazy people at my house, or do I...say, go to Cambridge Common and hear music."

He cawed twice and flew away.

There's my answer. Fly away with a song.

Before I left, I wrote one more letter.

August 18, 1974

Dear His Holiness the Dalai Lama,

You are really wise and I desperately need your advice. I don't want to live with my parents anymore. My father smacked me, Mom has a boyfriend even though they're still married. And other stuff. I'm sixteen and have one more year of high-school but I want to run away. I don't know why this is happening with my family. Any advice you can give me would be greatly appreciated.

Respectfully yours, JB

p.s. I meditate every day sometimes

CHAPTER SEVENTEEN: MAGIC ROCKS

In my room, I stuffed clothes in my bigger backpack with a toothbrush and a couple of books. Money was an issue and I hoped Mom had left some in the kitchen drawer. Why didn't I get a job this summer at Paragon Park? I would have made money and met new people. None of my friends worked—they went to camp, summer educational experiences, Maine, the Cape, Martha's Vineyard, Europe. Except Eric who sold weed. Were we all privileged? I didn't feel privileged. Some of my friends were rich, though I didn't think we were. It was strange, I had missed a whole section of life where you got a summer job, put your nose to the grindstone, made your own money— I hadn't even considered that.

My house was empty and I was surprised Mom wasn't setting up for her party, unless that was a front to get rid of me. After packing my stuff, I went looking for money and found three tens in the kitchen drawer. I took two, closed the drawer, opened it again and took the last ten. My note for Mom was short: *Meeting Amy in Cambridge, staying with her, see you tomorrow.*

It wasn't exactly a lie, that might happen, and Mom hadn't given me much of a choice.

There was a lock on my bike which I'd need. I hopped on and pumped fast, having no idea when the last ferry was. Dark shadows moved across the sky. I sped past the house by the bay with painted boulders that Rachel and I were intrigued with—we said sorcerers lived there. When Rachel and I used to ride our bikes past this house, we'd get the same feeling that mystical happenings were at play. The house was small and weather-beaten with thick support planks, a cement bay wall in back holding back the water. The boulders around the house were painted black, green, white, red, with strange artifacts such as masks and crosses wedged between them. Sculptures created from driftwood and rope were scattered between rocks, and it was said artists lived there, though Rachel and I knew they were witches. Every time we rode by we'd dare each other to touch a rock, and whoever touched it received magical powers for that day.

I wanted to stop and touch the rock but didn't want to miss the ferry so I rode on, past the old fort on the hill, the big houses on the cliff, and the library. Memories of summers past when Rachel, Mom and I went to the library every week, taking out hardback books with faded titles: *Little Women*, *Charlotte's Web*, *A Wrinkle in Time*, which I'd devour just like my penny candy. Those were better summers. When things weren't so messed up.

Two hills up and down an incline and I was by the high school across from the ferry. A boat was idling by the dock so I locked my bike, hurried to the window and bought a round-trip ticket. It was quiet here, the sound of water lapping against pilings, the snack bar that was attached to the ticket counter empty and dark.

There was an eerie feel to the night or maybe it was the uncertainty of my adventure.

As I stood by the dock, there seemed to exist that same beckoning towards something unseen, a connection between those painted rocks, a seagull's cry, the fog horn, this night full of the unknown.

A cool breeze blew, and I put on my sweatshirt as people exited the ferry. There was an older couple, the man pulling a red wagon filled with plants, two women with suitcases chatting animatedly, and a mom with a crying baby. A white bearded man who wore overalls took my ticket and I boarded.

The cabin of the boat had booths, individual seats and a bar in front. Upstairs was the deck and bridge where the captain sat. In my booth, there was a pile of leftover Sunday papers—*Boston Globe*, *Herald*, *Boston Phoenix*. The *Phoenix* music listings were in the back and Jack's had a band I didn't recognize. I wondered if Quinn would be there. The thought of him made me sad.

The Boston Globe had the Dear Abby column—I'd been checking our papers at home for her answer to my letter and so far, nothing. But there was a letter that caught my eye, from a sixteen-year-old in Portland, Maine. She wrote that her step-father stood over her bed when he thought she was asleep, put his hands under the sheet and touched her private parts. When this girl had told her mom, the mom said it was her imagination, and got angry at her. Just like mine did.

I wondered if her step-dad showed her Playboy magazine. Like my dad did.

When I was thirteen and started getting boobs, Dad would stare at my chest. I started rounding my shoulders so my boobs wouldn't show. Mine and Rachel's room was across from my parents, with Dad's closet in the hall. One morning when Dad was picking out his clothes, I passed by in my pajamas and Dad surprised me by pointing at my breasts. He poked them, lingering, like it was a game. "You're developing well," he had said, and smiled like it was an ordinary thing to do. A lump formed in my throat and I thought I was going to throw up. I remember wondering if he did that to Rachel. And said that she was developing well? Or was it just me, did I say something, walk a certain way to make Dad do that?

I was confused and felt ashamed like my body was doing bad things, asking for something I didn't want. Nothing else happened until about five months later when Dad was alone in the den, a wood paneled room with a big television set, two velvet chairs, a grey leather couch, built-in bookshelves, and a low wooden table by a window which housed a blown-glass candy dish that was usually empty. A cast-iron Buddha statue faced the couch on the floor—one of Mom's Bloomingdales purchases.

The encyclopedias were on the bottom shelf of the bookcase. That night, I needed the 'M' for a science report on monkeys. The news was on and Dad patted the couch. "Sit, Jezebel." He hadn't talked to me in a while, no questions about school, nothing. All he did was work, fight with Mom, eat dinner, watch television, and golf. So, I thought he was finally interested and we'd have a nice talk.

Dad had a magazine on his lap and as I sat he put the magazine between us. It was Playboy, which surprised me, since I had never seen that type of magazine in the house before. It was opened, and staring at us was a beautiful brunette woman, who wore short-shorts with an unbuttoned shirt, her enormous boobs popping from her bra with plenty of cleavage.

Dad spoke in a stern voice. "Don't you ever dress like that, Jezebel. Your bras should cover you, these reveal too much." He pointed at her breasts.

I thought she looked pretty sexy and I also wondered why he was showing me. Flashing in my mind was the day he touched my boobs in the hall. Unsure of what to say, an electric current ran through my body, freezing me, even though I wanted to jump up. As I studied the picture, he put his arm around me and stared at the television. My body stiffened as I thumbed through pages of sexy women who were pretty and made up with lots of their body parts exposed. I looked down at my own chest, comparing. Did I look like these playboy bunnies? As I turned the page, Dad put his hand on my thigh, it was ordinary, I remembered thinking, nothing really, until he moved it to my crotch and left it there.

The magazine fell as I jumped up. "I have homework," I said, running past Mom and Rachel in the kitchen to my bedroom. I turned off the light and stared into darkness, searching for an explanation.

The next day after school when Mom was ironing in the laundry room, I told her.

"Mom, Dad showed me Playboy magazine." I figured I'd start there and tell her the rest when she digested this, just to check her reaction.

Mom kept ironing a flowered cotton shirt that I had seen her wear the day before. "No, you're mistaken, it was Newsweek, or Time, we don't have Playboy in the house." She folded the arms and pressed the sleeves.

I put my hands on my hips. "Mom, it was Playboy, he showed me what kind of bra not to wear."

She shook her head and her mouth got tight. "It was nothing."

"Mom, it was weird."

Putting the iron down, properly so it didn't burn the fabric, Mom faced me. "Jezebel, no more stories! I've caught you lying before, and I won't have that. I'm going to have a cigarette." And she went upstairs to her bathroom where she did all her smoking.

It's true, I did lie. But I wasn't lying about this.

"He also touched my boobs," I said to the iron, because she was gone. Hiss, steam rising, burn. I believe you, Jez, the iron said.

Did he do the same thing to Rachel? She was constantly busy with internships, extra classes, her job at the bakery. I needed to tell her and was afraid, but after he did it again, I had to. I was caught off-guard, it was a month later and Dad said he wanted to talk, he hadn't paid me any attention so I thought…well I was stupid, wrong in thinking we would have a conversation, father to daughter. So, when he patted the cushion next to him on the couch, I sat. Mom was upstairs cleaning and Rachel was doing homework.

"Tell me what's going on," he had said. I sat an arms-length away, alert, but happy he seemed interested. He moved closer, put his arm around me, stared straight ahead at the evening news. Flashes of war scenes from Vietnam, the anchorman talking about American troops withdrawing, Operation Homecoming, an explosion in a field. Dad moved his hand and touched my boob on the side of my chest, his thumb moving up and down. Nonchalant, ordinary, as the anchorman described American casualties. There was a knot in my throat and it also felt sort of good which made me know something was very wrong with me. My brain told me to get up and my body disobeyed. Buddha statue stared at me, judgmental. I had seen other Buddha statues that laughed, smiled, seemed joyous, except ours was always serious, angry. Concerned.

Dad got up to use the downstairs bathroom. I jumped up and went upstairs, feeling guilty, gross, and wished I had a cigarette. Mom was still in the kitchen and I went into her bathroom and sniffed, there was smoke, she just had her after-dinner cigarette, so I opened the drawer to the sink and lit one of her Kents, sucking smoke down my lungs. Four puffs, then I flushed it and went into my bedroom.

Believing he cared about me, the happenings in my life, I fell into his trap again and it was confusing, infuriating. Yet it was the only time he noticed me, the only attention he gave me, and I hated how my body responded, turned-on, disgusting. I wanted to run out and have crazy sex with my boyfriend Eric and never be alone in a room with Dad again, for as long as I lived.

That winter snow was abundant, with drifts of white walls piled high. It was continuous, the cold, the snow. In my room, I stood by the window and watched snowflakes pour down like rain, thick, sticking instantly to the ground. Fast they fell, a dance, brisk, winter's gift, cover me, a blanket.

And then I told Rachel.

With her long, blonde hair up in a bun with pieces twisted by her neck, Rachel was a world away at her desk speed reading and highlighting.

"Dad touched me weird."

"Jez, what?" She put her book down and turned.

Far away a siren was screaming. Newton Wellesley Hospital, ambulance, police, an emergency.

"I was downstairs with him, just sitting, and he touched my boob like nothing was happening. He's done it before, Rachel, secret like he's not doing it. I thought he wanted to ask me about school or something."

Creases between her eyes deepened. "Dad wouldn't do that, Jez, his hand probably slipped." She turned back to her book.

"No, his hand didn't slip! He's done it before. And he stares at me not like a Dad should, you must know what I'm saying."

She turned a shade of red which told me, she knew. Maybe he did it to her too.

"Jez, I don't even know what to say. You've always lied about stuff, making up stories. It's not okay. Don't read those books anymore, they're making you oversexed."

Oversexed? This was my fault?

She motioned to my headboard where I kept my books, some I had borrowed from my parents—*Tropic of Cancer*, *Valley of the Dolls*, *Portnoy's Complaint*, next to my own current books—*The Hobbit*, *Native Son*, *Catcher in the Rye*, *Crime and Punishment*.

"It's not because of the books, Rachel, and I do tell the truth. No one listens or believes me, I'm telling you the truth now. Why would I make this up?"

"I don't think you're lying, really, just misinterpreting. I don't want to talk about it anymore, I have to study. Just forget it, don't keep saying it to anyone."

A few snowflakes stuck to the window, perfectly shaped. The world outside was beautiful, white, clean, pure.

Rachel was quiet and I didn't press. There was a fast burn tearing inside me.

That was the last time I said anything.

And one of the reasons I wrote those letters for advice. Was I making too much of it?

This was Dear Abby's answer to the girl from Portland.

Dear Scared in Maine,

First and most important, know that this is not your fault. You did nothing to cause this. Your step-father was wrong to touch you that way. Please find someone to talk with and tell them what happened. Perhaps at your school, or a counseling center. I'm sorry your mom doesn't believe you. I believe you.

There are many free clinics for counseling and I have included resources below. Your Stepfather has a sickness. See if you can get a lock on your door and remember, this is not your fault. The good and bad news is that you are not alone, I receive letters like yours all the time. Your first step was writing this letter.

At the end of the response, Abby left the name of counseling centers in Portland, and hot-line numbers.

Beyond the dirt-streaked window the black water was illuminated by distant lights of Logan Airport, with the noise of planes landing, taking off to places far away. The Boston cityscape was ahead.

Not her fault, Dear Abby said. *Talk with someone. She's not alone, free clinic. He's sick.*

I looked around at the people on the boat. The skinny dark-haired man with a mustache at the snack bar, did he have this experience, did his uncle touch him when they were changing into bathing suits one hot summer day? That big woman with black hair, acne, smoking furiously, was she molested by her older foster brother, the one her parents took in when she was eight? Abby wanted us all to feel better that we weren't alone but it didn't make me feel better, it just made me sadder.

And I didn't get, "it's not your fault". I knew it was creepy, disgusting, yet it must have been some message I gave that made Dad think it was okay to touch me, leer at me, treat me like I was something wrong.

The ferry was cruising to the dock and this night loomed large and empty. My plans for a reunion with Laura and Todd, who probably wouldn't remember me, or seeing Amy—those plans which in the light of day seemed so possible, now seemed illusive, a fantasy. What if no one was around? Where would I stay, what was I doing? Was this another mistake?

CHAPTER EIGHTEEN: ARJUNA

The boat docked and I walked down the ramp to an isolated downtown. I caught the T to Harvard Square and fifteen minutes later I was in front of the same phone booth as last night, in a similar predicament.

Amy's phone rang with no answer, Eric's phone rang, no answer. Bubbie? She'd love me to stay over, but it was too late and it might upset her. Summoning my inner Queen Jezebel, I asked silently, what do I do? Music drifted towards me mixed with laughter, so I followed the sounds to Cambridge Common.

There must have been a Harvard/Yale game because groups of students walked around wearing Logo tees carrying cases of beer and yelling, which gave the air a celebratory feel. Hunger and fatigue ran through my body. Food, must get food. The donut from this morning was a distant memory in my stomach.

Hare Krishna bells were the first sounds I heard. They were on the same side of the park as yesterday, their white van parked with people lined up at a long table for food. I made a bee-line there, walked past people on blankets, a trio on stage playing classical music.

I stood behind a man in a tattered and smelly army coat, and a Krishna woman with orange robes and long brown hair smiled at me as she put a spoonful of rice and some mushy vegetables on a paper plate.

"Roll?"

I was staring at the plate and glanced up. "Huh?"

"Do you want a roll, sugar?"

"Oh yes, please."

Her movements were graceful as she reached in a bag and handed me a small golden roll.

"Thank you." I moved to a patch of grass by their van, took off my sweatshirt to sit on, and ate. Army jacket man had taken his food to a bench, and sitting beside me on a wool blanket were a couple wearing identical floppy hats, laughing, kissing and eating rice. Hare Krishnas were circling the area, handing out pamphlets and asking people to take their book.

My food was gone quickly and even though it was tasteless, it made my stomach warmer and less hollowed. The night was cool with dark clouds and an August storm seemed to be brewing. Onstage a sonata was being played. There was a keyboard, flute, and violin. I wondered if they changed the line-up from jazz, and Laura and Todd wouldn't even be here. A fleeting thought that maybe Sparky would play tonight, in a jazz band, and I would finally ask him for lessons, made me hopeful. Then this wouldn't be a wasted, foolish adventure. It would be the culmination of all that I was seeking.

The Krishna woman was laughing with another woman and she came over and sat next to me.

"How are you?" She peered at me with her head tilted, probably thinking I was a runaway. I realized I could be anyone from anywhere, could be eighteen or twenty-one or a jazz musician.

"Great. I play jazz piano, going on tour soon—we just performed in Provincetown."

"Cool, look do you need a place to crash tonight?" She nodded at my backpack which I was leaning on, then back at me. She had this faraway quality in her eyes and I wanted to know her story, if she got recruited and if she would try to recruit me. I had heard about parents getting their children deprogrammed from cults. I didn't think the Hare Krishnas were a cult. Just that sometimes they found lost souls.

By my sneaker flies landed on a piece of zucchini.

She continued looking at me. "We have a place in Porter Square with tents in our backyard and you can have one of them tonight. If you help clean up." Handing me a large, plastic bag, I noticed she had an edge to her voice that I hadn't recognized before, and looking closer I realized she wasn't much older than me. Still, she had some kind of dreamy purpose.

I had nowhere else to go. Calling John was not an option. I already was a nuisance from last night and he wouldn't want to be my friend if he always had to rescue me.

"We'll split soon, after all the people get fed." She walked back to the serving table.

From the ground, I collected paper plates, napkins, and garbage. When no one was watching, I took two rolls, palmed them, and walked away. They were so small I ate them in three bites.

The crowd that sat on the lawn was older, not quite my parents age, and classical music still played. A bunch of younger guys and girls were by a bench, smoking a joint, and I gravitated towards them. A chubby girl in a halter top with butterflies tattooed on her shoulders gave me a glorious smile. "Want some chocolate mescaline?"

Mescaline was mellower than acid and didn't last as long, with no extremes, just a relaxed buzz. Practically like weed only better. She gave me one and I poured the capsule of Chocolate Nestle's Nesquik Powder mixed with mescaline on my tongue. As I handed her five dollars she gave me a joint plus a hug which I was grateful for, getting to see her butterflies up close as she pressed me against her flesh. If they had asked me to hang with them I might have, although they didn't, so I drifted back. The mescaline took hold quickly, bringing me to that comfortable place deep inside myself. Incense and cotton candy smells filled the air. The trees swayed and people walked past me in a blur.

The Krishnas had started a chant with cymbals playing, and I moved towards them as orange robes spun, floated, twirled.

"Last chant tonight everyone," said a Krishna man.

"Hare Krishna Hare Rama," I chanted, picking up cymbals and swaying. Everything shifted as I was carried along with this energy outside myself, stillness in motion. When the song was over, we all helped move stuff into vans, and then I was packed in the back seat of a red car, squished between four others, the couple on the blanket, army jacket guy who stunk of old liquor, and a youngish girl who sat on my lap. I pressed my face into her back to lessen the guy's stench.

In a moment of clarity I had an impulse to jump out of the moving car. Where was I going? I closed my eyes and crawled up inside myself to whatever safe corner was there.

Soon we pulled into a driveway behind a blue van and brought stuff into the house, a run-down structure with a porch. After a few trips, the Krishna girl led me to a backyard where there were some pup tents, a bonfire, and several metal lanterns with large thick candles aflame, lighting up a dirty and run-down yard. A few patches of grass were scattered by thick bushes, keeping it somewhat private from the house next door. It was pitch dark except for the fire.

"I have to pee," I said.

She led me through a back door to a bathroom near the kitchen where hundreds of orange robes were swaying, or maybe it was the mescaline.

"Use this bathroom. You can stay in the green tent, and let me know if you need anything. My name is Maya." Next she said a few sentences that all blurred together.

As I sat on the toilet, words buzzed through my brain. Green tent,

Maya, Hare Krishna Hare Rama. What were those sentences? Did she say, "I'll guide you into Krishnahood?" Was it, "Krishna loves you?" or, "I'm your friend?" Or perhaps it was just the bells I was hearing, or my own breath.

The backyard was dark. The folks from the car were sitting on large boulders by the fire and I joined them, taking off my back pack and leaning it against my leg, nervous someone might mess with my stuff. There was a hum of conversation and the hiss of wood burning. The young girl from the car was next to me. She had dirty blonde hair, wore a flannel shirt and jean shorts with hiking boots, and her legs seemed purple from the flames.

"So what's your name, where are you from?" Her eyes were wide open saucers as she grinned at me.

Again, I realized I could be anyone from anywhere. "My name is Jezebel, I live by the bay, my house has huge painted rocks that protect us. We're artists and magic happens at our home."

She smiled. "Wow, that's amazing." She pointed to the couple. "They're from Canada, I've never been there, have you? Anyway, are you going to join the Krishnas? I am."

I nodded since I didn't want to explain how I just needed a place to stay and was hungry.

"You don't join, Stephanie." The bad-smelling guy shot her a fierce look. "It's a practice. You dedicate your thoughts and actions to Lord Krishna and soon you get realized, you become God." His face was pale and thin, he had long, stringy dark hair, wore dirty jeans, heavy work boots, and was sitting erect and cross-legged yet at a strange angle, as if he might tip. "That's what we're supposed to say to new people, didn't you read the pamphlet?"

Stephanie looked down at her feet and shrugged. "I'm joining," she mumbled.

"That's really cool," I said, feeling bad he jumped down her throat. "Hey, do you know which green tent is mine?" I stood, wanting away from the man's vibes that were making me uneasy. Also, the weed in my pocket beckoned. I knew that Hare Krishna's didn't do drugs, so discretion was important if I didn't want to get kicked out.

Stephanie followed me with a lantern. "Here, light your way."

"Cool." There were three green tents, so I popped my head in the first one. The smelly guy yelled that that was his tent so buzz off. It was surprising. All the Krishna people I had met so far were nice, so I figured he was just a mean drifter.

The second green tent was empty save for a sleeping bag in the corner. I took off my backpack as Stephanie gave me the lantern.

"Hey do you want to smoke a joint with me?"

Stephanie leaned close and there was a tiny painted flower by her right cheek bone. "I'll be a real Krishna soon so I'm not smoking anymore. Also, I'm a vegetarian!" Her eyes sparkled as she put her hands together in a prayer.

"That's great, you found your path." I meant it, too, and hugged her. She seemed so sweet and hopeful. Stephanie waved and ducked beneath the flap.

The no-see-ums above my head made a pattern which I watched for a bit, then took two clam shells from my bag and my new sea glass, arranging them by the lantern. There was a long red scratch on my mosquito bite arm, from elbow to wrist, and I stared at the design it made, a wavy line followed by bumps. My leg scratches from Amherst had dissolved with all my ocean swims.

Outside was quiet with occasional snaps of wood.

Faraway, I thought I heard a saxophone playing and piano keys. I wondered if that was Sparky or my musician friends performing but realized there was no way music from the common could travel this far. My mouth was dry and I had no supplies. I wandered outside toward the house. Someone had put more logs in the fire and it was blazing. Shapes from candles danced in the tents with the rustle of people settling in for a night's sleep.

In the kitchen, a Krishna man sat at the table drinking tea, reading a book, a dim lamp beside him. As I entered the room he smiled and closed his book. His bright blue eyes made me realize he was the man I fell in love with that day on Boston Common, with Amy.

"Hey, I know you. You were at Boston Common a few weeks ago."

Nodding, he said, "Sure. That's one of the places we feed people." He wore a Red Sox baseball hat, loose white pants with a thin, cotton tee, and was muscular and gorgeous. His eyes smiled with light. I wanted to get closer and let whoever he was rub off on me.

"Do you want some tea?" He went to the stove where a kettle was still steaming.

"Yes, that would be excellent."

"You're funny." Pouring water over a teabag, he smiled as he placed it on the table. "What's your name?"

"Jezebel."

"Ah, powerful name. Very spiritual."

The tea turned a strange greenish color, unlike Mom's black tea, and it emitted a spicy aroma. "I'm searching for answers to a million questions."

He asked me if that was why I was drawn to the Krishna's, and I didn't answer, just considered his question. I was drawn here because they were nice, I was hungry, and something else undefinable.

Finally I said, "I'm not sure."

He nodded and we sipped our tea.

"What's your name?"

"Arjuna."

"That's your real name?"

Laughing, he said, "That's what I go by."

The tea tasted of green grass and oranges, and I watched the steam swirl around in a relaxed pattern. Since Krishnas were wise and spiritually knowledgeable, I thought this man-boy might help me if I told him everything. If I said, Mom drinks all the time and has a boyfriend, my father molested me and no one believes me, what should I do? Would he tell me to join the Hare Krishnas, help them sell the books, become a vegetarian, get up early, not do drugs or party? Would he tell me, find Sparky, get your life together, forget about your family? Alongside my urge to confess another one surfaced—the desire to curl up on his lap, kiss his clean-shaven face, and see his eyes laughing over me.

Moving my hand, I touched his fingers and his arm, feeling his soft skin. He raised his eyebrows with a smile and stood up.

"Time for sleep." With a curious expression, he titled his head and gazed at me.

"Can we hug goodnight, are you allowed?"

There was a pause. And then he reached for my hand, held it warmly. "Jezebel, the temptress. We're celibate you know unless we're married."

"Let's get married!"

As he laughed, I realized he was older than I first judged by exquisite little lines on the side of his eyes. Holding my gaze, he said, "Jezebel. Don't mistake your very powerful spiritual energy as sexual energy. Contain it."

I pictured a huge glass storage unit that held all the guys I had sex with, all the kisses, blowjobs, sweaty embraces. I didn't understand what he meant, although I liked the way he said it, like he was giving me some kind of gift.

He walked away—a sage, confident and detached.

In the backyard, I lingered by the fire, thinking about what he said. Be contained.

And what John had said. Take pause.

I so wanted this wisdom. Needed to learn it. Learn everything. How to manage in this world, with my family, other people. Become someone new. Become someone better, take all these lessons and immerse them into my being. No more bad decisions. These people were true, smart. Dear Abby said to confide in someone. Who? John? Quinn? Stephanie, Arjuna?

The bag lady by the swan boats on Boston Common?

The bonfire flared high. Lanterns flickered in the tents, and the mescaline faded, making my mind slow. Not remembering which tent was mine, I headed towards a green one, opened the flap, ducked in, and saw the smelly guy sitting on his sleeping bag shirtless, a bottle of Jim Beam in his hand. At first he glared, then his expression changed to a half-smile.

"Come to visit me?"

"No, sorry, wrong tent."

"Want some whiskey?"

"No, thanks." Quickly, I ducked out. Another green tent was near and I crawled in, found my shells lined up in a row, the lantern still on. Sitting cross-legged on the hard dirt, I closed my eyes and tears rolled down my cheeks. I wished I was home in my bed with familiar sounds of the ocean, wind, the fog horn. Scared of this long night ahead, I saw the candle flicker and hoped it would stay lit all night. Darkness made me afraid ever since I was five and a babysitter turned off the hall light and I had a nightmare about bad things crawling in the dark. It was one of those recurring nightmares that took different forms as I got older.

Eventually sleep would come. Maybe in the morning I would meet Sparky if I went to Berklee second floor on my way to the ferry. See Quinn. The thought calmed me and I made up a story in my head where Sparky was my teacher, I got really good at piano, famous, and lived happily ever after. With Quinn, of course.

CHAPTER NINETEEN: STEPHANIE'S HATS

I couldn't sleep. My tent was musty and the air had a chill like a storm was brewing, with sudden changes in temperature, unlike any August weather I remembered. There were times at the beach when my sister and I watched August storms arrive. They first appeared in the swells of the waves, and then electrical wires on the poles snapping crazily with increasing winds, and finally long, sharp bolts of lightning which we viewed from the safety of our front porch.

I wished she was with me. That she had been with me all summer. I wouldn't be here in this cold tent.

In my pack was a hooded sweatshirt which I struggled over my head, tying the hood under my chin. Heat from the bonfire beckoned, and I crept outside. There was a pile of wood by the bushes. I loaded my arms, threw logs in the fire, and watched flames blaze high, the heat warming my body. Time was lost. Was it midnight, three a.m., would this night drag on with its chill? Sleepless minutes felt too long, and I hoped daylight would come soon.

Then what. Then what.

This wasn't a very good idea, coming here to this camp with strangers. My choices were all wrong.

A long stick protruded from the fire, its end red-hot and glowing, resembling a car lighter. The joint butterfly girl gave me. It was squished in my side pocket and I retrieved it, held it to the stick's end and inhaled, tasting the sweet flavor of weed. This might help me sleep or retrigger the mescaline, either way it was something. I blew smoke in the air, looked up at the windows of the house and wondered which room was Arjuna's. I imagined sneaking into his room and crawling in bed with him.

The thought of it made me laugh.

"What's funny?"

A voice came from behind and I turned to see smelly guy outside his tent, his eyes on me. Holding his bottle of whiskey, he was a sorry interruption which I wanted to ignore, although I could smell him, mold and vomit. A vision of the man at the farmhouse flashed before me. Fear ran through every cell in my body.

Queen Jezebel what would you do? She whispered on the screen of my mind. I am powerful, spiritual, a phoenix, anyone from anywhere. Magic stones are in my pocket. I am Queen Jezebel of desert winds.

He sat on a boulder near me, and reached for my weed which I gave him. He held up his bottle and I shook my head.

He moved the bottle until it almost touched my face. "Come on, girly, Krishnas share everything."

His eyes were dark coals feasting on me, and I wanted to poke them with the red-hot end of my stick. Don't stare, mister, I will blind you. He slipped off the boulder and righted himself, an unsteady motion, and my body stiffened, alert, ready.

"Girly you have to open your heart like a fart." Laughing at himself, his speech was garbled and too loud for the quiet of the night, alarming. "That's an inside joke. I can teach you a lot, I'm inaugurated, I mean, high up, a person for you to know. How about you come to my tent, I'll open you up, ha-ha."

The words he spoke traveled to a part of me that was wide awake, watchful, and a danger sign flashed. This wasn't Grey orating a funny illusion at our acid party, or someone who smoked too much weed. This was something else, an unnatural darkness.

Shifting so he faced me, I focused on the fire, its power. The embers, hot, sharp, protective. He got up swaying, unbalanced, and unzipped his fly.

"Watch this girly."

He pissed into the fire, a long arch, and grinned as he made sure I watched. The wood sizzled, the scent of urine mixed with smoke as he turned, his penis dangling from his jeans as he thrust his hips back and forth, making some vile sound.

I stood and aimed the lit end of my stick at him. "Get away."

He was unsteady as he put his bottle on the ground and moved towards me. As his hand grabbed for me, I jabbed the searing end of the stick into his palm. Screaming, he pulled away. I waved the stick at his body and he lunged, banged his body against me, his penis still hanging from his jeans. Jamming the stick into his arm I pushed him with my hip, he felt weightless in his stupor, he was an insect, a pest. Tripping over a boulder, he fell backwards into the fire as a look of surprise flashed across his face, which changed to terror as flames embraced him.

He screamed, "Help me, you bitch, I'm burning, help!"

A strong smell, rotten meat burning. I took a step backwards away from this darkness that emanated like poison. His jeans were aflame, and he scrambled on his hands and knees out of the fire, doing some odd dance to extinguish the flames. The Canadian man scrambled from his tent, assessed what was happening, and yelled for his lady to get a blanket. The darkened house turned bright as people woke. I took two more steps back until I was behind the bushes, hidden.

The guy flailed his arms with sparks flying, as the Canadian woman threw a blanket around his legs. Her boyfriend threw water all over him, panicked. The guy screamed, jumped, and suddenly, as if he was a dry, old tree, he tipped, falling with a loud thud as his head hit something. He rolled once, twice, then stilled, the only sound the sizzle of water on coals, or skin, and crickets in trees. Chirp chirp, their innocent song.

Stephanie left her tent and ran to the guy as the couple knelt beside him. "What happened, what happened? Call an ambulance, oh my God, he's dead!"

Maya came from the house wearing shorts and a tee-shirt, followed by a Krishna guy wearing an orange bathrobe. Moving further into the bushes, my mind was frozen. Smoke hissed from my stick, still lit in my hand. Evidence.

An ambulance arrived. Police came. Fire engines came. Questions were asked and I listened as Canadian man told police that the guy was drunk and fell, it was obvious, he reeked of liquor and urine and badness. His head was split, his body burned, and they took him away in a blare of sirens and lights.

Maya begged a police officer not to evict them, she promised no more bonfires or tents. The fire was extinguished and they all went into the house. Arjuna stood on the back steps and his gaze swept the backyard. Was he searching for me? I didn't move. I was a stone, a painted rock, blue sea-glass. I was waiting for some magic.

Some of the trees were evergreens and they had a pine smell to them, strong and refreshing. Pressing my face against the wood, I wished I could crawl through the bark, become a squirrel.

Help me, tree, please help me.

What had I become? Was I strong? Or was this the most terrible thing? A thing that had to be erased like an etch-a-sketch, shake the board clear. Paint a quiet picture from years past: me on the beach with my boogie board, Rachel beside me reading, Mom nearby playing scrabble with friends, Dad at home watching the football game eating Planters dry roasted peanuts.

The house lights went off and the Canadian couple headed to their tent, followed by Stephanie who was almost skipping as if buoyed by some new knowledge. She opened the flap of her tent and crawled in.

The wind blew cold and I was freezing. From behind the trees I walked out slowly, glancing at the fire that had wisps of black smoke curling around the air. The place where he fell was smoothed over with no signs of turmoil.

Stephanie's lantern was lit and she was still awake. "Stephanie, it's Jezebel, can I come in?"

Sounds of movement. "Yes, where have you been?"

Inside, Stephanie was in her sleeping bag which was zipped up to her neck. Wearing a knit hat with her hair in pigtails, she looked about ten-years-old. There was a dusty wool blanket beside the lantern.

"Can I use that blanket, I'm freezing."

As I put the blanket over me, Stephanie reached into her sleeping bag and tossed me a knit hat with a white pom-pom. I put it on and curled up next to her.

"Thanks for the hat."

"My mom knit it. She knits everything—hats, sweaters, blankets. Just sits and knits and chews spearmint gum."

Stephanie lay on her side facing me. "So you missed everything. The creepy guy fell into the fire, cracked his head and got burnt, his dick was hanging from his pants."

I nodded like this was new information. She continued. "We guessed he went for a piss and fell, since he was drunk, stinking of liquor. His legs caught fire and everything. How did you not hear? Anyway, tents come down tomorrow, which ends up great for me because Maya said I can move into the house and wear a Krishna robe. It's sort of like a promotion." She removed a plastic container from her sleeping bag and drank. "Want some water?"

"Thanks." After drinking big, thirsty gulps, I said, "What about the guy?"

"Well, if he dies he'll just be reincarnated, probably as a dog, which would be a step up, dogs are cool. Maya said she'll call the hospital tomorrow. Where did you go?"

"Just walked around."

Stephanie unzipped her bag when she noticed my shivering. "Come snuggle, two is warmer. And everyone gets up wicked early so we need to sleep."

Climbing into the warm flannel, her body emanated a comforting heat. My feet touched clothes and containers, and she explained that she kept all her stuff in the bag for when she needed it during the night. As I snuggled to her back, she zipped up the bag, and instant warmth comforted, like a hot bath on a winter night. Quiet overwhelmed me and tears filled my eyes. Just the smell of Stephanie, oranges and soap, made me realize what awfulness just happened. Tears ran down my face as I held back sobs.

Her hand reached mine and she held me. "You okay? You miss your mom?"

"I'm okay." Stephanie's breath became even and her hand fell away as I nestled against her back. My tears continued to fall, unstoppable with this new quiet. Soon even crickets were silent as we drifted away, together into a vast green ocean of sleep.

CHAPTER TWENTY: OATMEAL AND CHAI

The sound of gongs, resounding and deep, woke me. Everything was confused. Was I dreaming, where was I? My eyes opened as a soft voice said, "That's the breakfast gong, we need to be on time."

I remembered. Cambridge, Stephanie, tent, Hare Krishnas. Fire, guy, death.

Stephanie retrieved her toothbrush and toothpaste from a make-shift shelf, and I reached for my pack. The stick from last night jutted out from the pocket. The weapon, my protection against the guy who might be dead. The familiar sight of my books, clothes, and pens made me crave home, and I stuck my head in the pack, wanting to disappear into somewhere ordinary.

"Come on," Stephanie said, moving fast.

I followed her into the cold morning holding my toothbrush, my breath steamy in the air, August turning suddenly cool. Inside, Maya was by the stove. She stirred a huge steaming pot and filled bowls as Krishnas brought their breakfast to a long, wooden table. Yummy aromas emanated and Stephanie handed me a mug of steaming tea and a bowl of thick oatmeal. She said the tea was called Chai, and after a sip, I decided it was the best thing I ever tasted, milky and sweet with an unidentifiable spice giving it a kick.

I joined the table and didn't look at anyone. I wondered if they knew it was me who killed the guy. The oatmeal was thick and creamy with cinnamon and brown sugar and so so delicious. The thought that I'd join the Hare Krishnas just because of their breakfast made me smile. People were eating in silence so I figured it was a thing. It didn't seem to matter how much you ate, although I noticed Hare Krishnas ate frugally, with half bowls and half pieces of the fresh bread that was in the middle of the table. I took two pieces, glanced around and spotted Arjuna across the table. He smiled at me and I felt ashamed at the two large pieces of bread in my hand, but it didn't stop me from eating them. I hadn't seen a fat Hare Krishna yet, just skin and bones under the robes, although Arjuna was buff. He probably lifted weights and did other regular things, and I thought it would be cool to know him, become life-long buddies. He'd visit me in jail after they arrested me.

Three gongs sounded and everyone closed their eyes, so I pretended to close mine and watched as people prayed. I needed a prayer. Please help me be smarter, help gross smelly guy not be dead, help me listen to Arjuna and contain myself. Help me take pause like John taught me. Help me find my way. There were a lot of things I could ask for.

Someone chanted "Hare Om," and everyone else chanted back, it went this way for a few minutes, back and forth. When the chant ended a man stood up. He had smooth Black skin, short dark hair except a long braid down his back and he wore the orange robes. People beamed at him with adoration. With brown eyes that were clear and bright, I imagined he was a good person for discussions about the meaning of life. I bet he'd have a sense of humor, since his eyes seemed filled with laughter.

He had a deep, soft voice. "Hello folks, just a few announcements before we start the week, happy Monday. Green van will be going to Logan Airport, Devi will be leading, white van to Boston Common, Arjuna will be leading. We hope to feed lots of folks today and of course, spread the message. Maya contacted the hospital and will give her report. No more tents or fires from today on, and Stephanie will be joining us in the house. Welcome, Stephanie."

Squeezing my hand, Stephanie's face lit up. People around the table nodded and smiled, and I was happy for her. As Maya stood to give her report, my stomach lurched. Please please please please.

"The hospital person said Derek, he's the guy who showed up two days ago, needed ten stitches on his head and had minor leg burns. Police reported that he didn't remember what happened, wasn't pressing charges and was going back to his home state of New Hampshire."

He didn't remember what happened and was alive. I felt my breath release.

Maya continued. "The cops gave us a warning. No bonfires, tents or vagrants, although, weren't we all vagrants at one time? When I lived…"

The Krishna man cleared his throat and stood back up. "Thank you so much for your report, Maya." She sat down, her face beet red.

"Have a great day everyone, see you tonight! Hare Krishna!" The man bowed his head and people got up with their dishes. Stephanie collected all the dishes around her and danced over to the sink while people welcomed her into the house.

I went over with my bowl. "Need help?"

She shook her head and whispered, "A good first impression is important. Get your stuff together, you can work Logan with us!"

There was no way I was working at Logan Airport with the Krishnas. I had to get home. I felt sick, and needed my sister, salt water, my shells, sun, my bike Aragorn. Even Mom. Stephanie was a sweet girl and I felt our connection, maybe because I heard her steady breath last night, the heat from her body creating a soft, safe nest. I wanted happiness for her, that she be okay, forever okay.

In the bathroom, I peed and brushed my teeth. I had to poop but didn't want to leave a smell. There was a stick of incense and matches, probably left for that purpose, so I lit the incense, did my business, and washed my hands. The shower looked inviting although I didn't want to linger. My armpits smelled okay, just smoky. I ran the incense under water and went to change. When I had one sleeve through my flannel shirt, Arjuna walked over, wearing his Red Sox hat, orange robes, and black high top Converse sneakers.

"You taking off, Miss Jezebel?"

"Yeah." There was no one else at the table. "Arjuna, can I tell you something?"

"Sure."

He waited for me to talk. A serene smile on his face was my invitation to trust him.

I took a deep breath. "The guy who was drunk last night, Derek. He was bothering me. I poked him with a stick that was hot from the fire and it burned him. He kept bothering me so I pushed him into the fire and his pants lit and then he fell, smashed his head, got hurt. It was because of me."

Arjuna's blue eyes dulled as he travelled somewhere far away, a crystal ball, somewhere I couldn't access.

"Okay. Let me get this straight. You defended yourself against a drunk, unruly man, and you think it's your fault?"

My eyes filled with tears. "Oh, okay. I thought…"

"Jezebel." He took my hand. "There's a great Indian epic, the Mahabharata, and within this story there is a battle, which represents the struggle between our inner and outer selves, between light and dark. The most important quest. The story speaks about being a warrior, courage in the face of adversity, and how to find your righteous path. Your own inner truth. Like what your name stands for: courage, fearlessness. You absolutely did the right thing. You protected yourself."

That is what happened. What Arjuna said was the truth, it was protection. I was strong like Jezebel.

"You're a seeker," Arjuna said. "Nothing is wrong with you, in fact, you're very precious. Keep searching and you'll find that what you seek is closer than you'd ever guess."

The door opened and a few Hare Krishnas walked upstairs, glancing our way but not stopping.

Precious. Courageous. Arjuna noticed parts of me that I always thought had to be hidden. The fierceness. Curiosity. I believed those parts were weird and he made me see myself in a new way.

"Arjuna, how did you get so wise?"

He smiled. "Life is a great teacher, Jezebel. We'll have a cup of tea sometime and I'll tell you my story, through dark forests and sunny mountain tops."

Darkness and light. I loved this man. "I hope I see you again."

Opening his arms, he gave me a warm hug, smelling like incense and cinnamon. I pressed my face against his robes, wanting his goodness.

"You know where to find me," he said, and walked out to start his day.

Stephanie was still at the sink, humming and washing. "Stephanie. Thanks so much for everything."

She wiped her hands and gave me a big hug. "Next time you see me I'll be wearing an orange robe and living in the house! Make sure you visit, okay?"

As I walked out the front door, sadness crept over me leaving Stephanie and Arjuna. They were really good people and I felt their kindness had altered me.

Last night's chill had settled deep. I shivered, my body uncomfortable with an aroma of fire and dirt. Arjuna said I wasn't wrong, but I couldn't shake the feeling that it was awful, another bad choice.

Rain was steady as I walked city sidewalks with soaked feet, the cuffs of my jeans drenched, dampness pressing my skin. Wind whipped off tall downtown buildings. A big clock on an old brick church said

10:30. Its wooden doors were tall, heavy, held open with huge round stones, an invitation to enter.

Inside were huge cathedral ceilings, stained glass windows with faces, patterns. Jesus on the cross. Footsteps echoed on the tile floor, tap tap tap. Candles flickered, someone was kneeling and prayers were being whispered.

In this church, there was a presence. I had fake prayed with the Krishnas. Who do I pray to? Dear Abby, Timothy Leary, Dalai Lama, God? Dad was an atheist, Mom was embarrassed to talk about it, the meditation book said there was a higher self within me. Hare Krishnas prayed to Lord Krishna, Jezebel worshipped her own Gods and Goddesses, people prayed to Jesus. So many different beliefs. What was mine? The acid trip showed me stars, galaxies, the vast expanse of a night sky with thousands of glimmers.

There was a low, padded desk in one of the back rows which I knelt on. I whispered, "Dear higher source, God, whoever you are, forgive me for the guy last night and help me."

Rain pattered high above and a breeze blew in from the open doors. A priest stood by a cubicle, glancing around. Our eyes met and I looked away. Forgive me Father for I have sinned. I pushed a man into fire, faked my age at clubs, went to a farmhouse with a strange man and almost got raped and killed. I hate my parents, my father molested me and Mom has a boyfriend. I want to run away. Forgive me Father. Help me.

The priest walked down the aisle to the front of the church and disappeared. I wondered if Jews could do confession. What if I pretended I was Catholic? The priest would give me advice, tell me which special prayers to repeat. Lost, I'm lost, I would say, I have too many secrets. Go home, child, he'd say.

On the way out there was a table with cards that had prayer hands and the words, "The Kingdom of Heaven is within." A tray next to the cards had money for donations and I gave a dime, took a card and stuck it in my pocket. Outside, people hurried along the sidewalk. An old man begged in a tattered wheel chair underneath the green awning of an Italian restaurant. A broken umbrella flapped in the gutter, it's spokes sticking skyward.

Across the street was a music store. My music lessons. Sparky— totally forgotten in the haze of last night. I crossed the street and looked in the window at instruments, song books, posters of musicians. Seeing my reflection was awful— hair knotted, streaks of dirt on my face, feet filthy from two days in flip flops. I buttoned up my shirt, smoothed my hair, brushed off my jeans, cleaned some dirt off my feet with a tee-shirt and adjusted my back pack.

Inside was warm, dry and quiet with rows of music books and sheet music. Towards the back were guitars, flutes, saxophones, percussion instruments and electric keyboards. Two men at the counter bent over some papers and glanced at me, nodded, and went back to their work.

Gershwin, Billie Holiday, Ella Fitzgerald, Duke Ellington, Nina Simone, Broadway musicals, thick books with glossy covers. I opened a book, remembering the chords Shannon taught me and how great it felt to jam with everyone in Provincetown. Like I was a part of the music scene.

In the back near the drum sets was a bulletin board with flyers and business cards, and one caught my eye: "JAZZ PIANO LESSONS, AFFORDABLE". Her name was Ana Rodriquez and I jotted down the number, promising myself I'd call when I got home.

At the ferry, a ticket lady with bluish hair and a thick Boston accent told me the next boat was arriving in ten minutes. I huddled under the waiting area, a chill shaking my body, wishing for a warm, sunny day, hot sand below my feet, even Mom's laugh when she was tipsy.

Just as the lady said, the ferry came ten minutes later. I handed my ticket to a woman wearing army green overalls who looked similar to the stocky man from yesterday. She even had a little beard. She examined the front and back of my ticket a few times, scowled, and stepped aside.

At the snack counter, I bought some hot tea and slid into a booth.

When I stopped shivering, I took my things from my backpack and placed them on the table. The clothes were damp and some pages were curled on my books. *The Prophet*, *Siddhartha*. That night in the car with my parents, the last time we were all out together, their fight, when I had decided to become a jazz piano player. It was only two months ago in June and it seemed so long ago, a dream ago.

I put my head on the table, closed my eyes, and let the water rock me. The words of Arjuna and John buzzed in my brain along with my own thoughts. Nothing is wrong with you, you're beautiful, strong, creative, courageous, not wrong, not bad. It's not your fault, it is my fault, nothing is wrong with you, everything is wrong with me.

Ten minutes later, the ferry horn sounded and I got up to watch our arrival in the fog. We docked and I ran to the bike stand, to my trusty, black bike Aragorn. As I felt the familiar softness of the leather seat, more tears filled my eyes. Wait till I tell you what happened, Aragorn, you're not going to believe it.

The rain had slowed to a mist and I rode past the library, the fort, past the witches' house with the painted boulders, past sand dunes on Beach Ave. Places inside me that I didn't even realize were in knots relaxed.

Riding up my street I looked for Mom's car by the curb and was relieved it wasn't there. I didn't want to listen if she needed to talk and didn't want to talk if she asked questions. The house was sparkling clean, as usual, with no remnants of a party which puzzled me. Mom wanted me gone for some reason, and it was all her fault I nearly killed a guy.

In my room, slipper shells, blue mussels, half clams, smooth stones greeted me. Hi, friends, I'm home, you wouldn't believe what happened. I took off my clothes and took the hottest, longest shower of my life, scrubbing all streaks of dirt with ivory soap and washing my hair with Herbal Essence. The knots in my hair didn't untangle. For that I would need Rachel. I'd call tomorrow, tell her it was an emergency and she had to come home immediately.

Wrapped in a fluffy, yellow towel, I crawled into crisp, clean sheets. I inhaled the flowery smell of my pillow as I pulled a blue cotton blanket over my head, digging myself far under the blankets to disappear the chill that had overtaken me.

CHAPTER TWENTY-ONE: MUSIC TO THE RESCUE

For the next three days I stayed in bed, coughing and sneezing. I dreamt of fire and smoke, and one dream of the guy's face that made me sit up in bed. I made promises to myself. I would do better. I had to change my ways.

Mom was always good when Rachel or I were sick and this was no exception. She brought me hot tea, grilled cheese sandwiches, cough medicine, my inhaler, juice, and Betty and Veronica comic books which I had outgrown though they comforted me all the same.

On the fourth day, I forced myself to get up. It was noon and the house was quiet. I made some tea and sat on the front steps with my cup. This was Thursday of the last weekend before Labor Day so the beach would be crowded. It was a three H day: hazy, hot and humid. My neighbor Edith waddled from her house to mine holding a china plate loaded with sugar cookies.

"I heard you had a summer cold which is lousy, so I brought you home baked sugar cookies. You know the saying, dear, feed a cold, starve a fever."

She was so earnest and concerned. Edith was what I pictured when I imagined typical mothers—matter-of-fact, confident in their role as homemaker, disciplining the children in a firm yet kind manner.

Edith's children were grown and she had grandkids that she probably spoiled in just the right way.

The plate was warm and sweet aromas made my stomach growl. "Thank you."

Glancing upward, she said, "It's going to be a scorcher today, Jezebel. Let the sun bake away the rest of your cold. Don't swim." She walked at a slow steady pace back to her house. The cookies were warm and chewy and I had four of them in quick succession. An ice cream truck rode by, rang its bell, and I relaxed as the heat of the sun warmed my face.

So much had happened the past week for me to understand.

Mom pulled up in her car with bags of groceries and a tight expression, and as I helped put groceries away, she sighed. "I don't know why I bother, there's only ten more days left. The end of summer is terrible."

"I'm making more tea, want some Mom?" I filled the kettle and sneezed three times.

"Barry's going to his other house today and we were partners in a card game so I have to find someone else. Everyone is talking about packing, moving back. This is the worst part of summer."

Now you know how I felt all summer, Mom. And by the way, my cold is getting better, thanks for asking. And care to hear about my adventures with the Hare Krishnas? I pictured how Mom would react if I told her—an overwhelmed, glazed look on her face, asking, "Isn't that a cult?" Or maybe she'd be kind, though I couldn't risk it. It was just too big, my mistake, and I wanted it gone from my memory.

The kettle whistled. I turned it off and decided instead of tea I would hit the beach. I put on my bikini and grabbed my bag. The road was hot but my bare feet were tough from walking all summer without shoes.

On the beach were my favorite sounds. The distant whine of songs from radios, kid's happy yells, the low mumble of conversations, waves breaking. I buried my hands and feet into hot sand and fell into a half-sleep, opening my eyes when my body felt like fire. I'm going to die of heat stroke, splayed on the sand. Turn into a shell, a starfish.

Dizzy, I walked to the water's edge and dove through a wave. The cool, dark green water surrounded me, gulls were overhead and my body floated over waves. Thick clouds were fast moving, holding images in grey and pink. The ferry, piano keys, Mom's hat. Tears.

Maybe everything was simpler than I thought. Stephanie with her sweet voice, orange robes, her sleeping bag stuffed with all her possessions. Arjuna's advice to be contained. John's wisdom. Eating a sleeve of cookies, hiding in bed. Queen Jezebel's strength. Becoming a feminist. Rocks on the beach, riding my bike with no hands. Music. Being happy.

After floating, I walked a slow pace home. Mom and Barry were on the porch with cocktails and cigarettes. I guess he came back from his other house early. I had an urge to scream, "you leather-faced wife stealer," except I felt bad because Mom was happy again. They were going to an end-of-summer party, Mom said, there were cold-cuts in the fridge. Everything was an end-of-summer event; end-of-summer trip to the grocery store, end-of-summer card game. It felt unnecessary.

When they left, I made a plate of corned beef and turkey and took one of my dad's Miller beers out of the fridge. I drank half the bottle quickly, and felt a little buzzed. The corned beef was salty and with mustard, it tasted great. After the first beer I got another, took one of Mom's Kent cigarettes from the drawer, and as the sun started its descent I pretended to be in a movie.

Turning to the cameras I said out loud, "Yes, darling, I'm so excited for our trip overseas, of course we'll do Paris first." Puff of my cigarette. "No museums this time, just galleries, we'll visit Francois on the west bank, and jazz clubs, of course."

Jazz clubs! This was a perfect time to call Ana Rodriquez. I dug through my backpack which reeked of bonfire smoke and found her number. The prayer hands card fell out with the saying, *The Kingdom of Heaven is Within*, reminding me of that morning in the church. I stuck the card under a napkin and decided I would practice the phone conversation.

"Hello, Miss Rodriquez? Hello, Ana Rodriquez? Hi, Ana?" My voice was low and mature. I dialed the number.

A woman answered, "Hello?"

"Hi is Ana Rodriquez there?" My voice sounded high and babyish.

"Just a minute, please."

I cleared my throat and took a gulp of beer, which didn't calm my nerves.

The woman yelled, "Sparky, phone!"

My head spun. What did she say?

"Hello, this is Ana." Her voice was deep and rich, slow.

"Hi, I'm calling about piano lessons. I saw your card at a music store downtown."

There was a pause. "Presently I'm full, I can give you other names."

No matter how it sounded, I had to ask. "Um, did she call you Sparky?"

Ana laughed. "That's my stage name."

Sitting upright I knocked over my beer and didn't even care. "I can't believe it's you, I've been searching for you all summer! The lead singer at Jack's told me to find you!"

"Do you remember who it was?"

Feeling my courage falter, I pushed myself. After all this, I was talking with Sparky! "She had thick red hair and was playing with a man with six fingers."

Sparky gave a hearty laugh. "Well, that's a different story, honey, that must have been Hound Dog's band. I can make room for you. What's your deal, are you a college student?"

"I'm sixteen, almost a senior in high school."

"That's great, it's good to start young. What's your name?"

"Jezebel."

"Great stage name, darling." There was a pause as I heard paper shuffling. "Can you come on Monday at one? Second floor studio at Berklee, downtown. Fifteen dollars for students."

Berklee downtown! Magic words to my ears. Yes I knew where that was, yes I could afford fifteen dollars, and yes I would see her on Monday.

Dancing around the living room I sang, "Ana Rodriquez is Sparky, Ana Rodriquez is Sparky!" I danced in the kitchen, danced for my shells, danced until I collapsed on the couch in the dark with a smile plastered ear-to-ear. I waved to the cameras, pressed my face into the pillow and screamed. Ana Rodriquez is Sparky. And I had a lesson with her, this Monday!

CHAPTER TWENTY-TWO: BALL CASTLE

The next day Mom went to visit Rachel and shop for college. "I'll be back before six, Jez. There's an end-of-summer porch party at Barry's." She stopped scurrying around and stirred sugar into her tea, her mouth in a frown. For the past week whenever she said Barry's name she got sad.

"At least our family will be back to normal with Dad around and all," I said, not really believing it myself. I hadn't missed their fights and all the weirdness with my dad.

Her voice was far away. "I might just stay here an extra few weeks."

I didn't answer, there was no point. Poor Mom, she just didn't see what was happening. She couldn't see past herself. Sometimes I hated she was so oblivious.

It was a crowded Saturday on the beach even though it was cloudy. I put my stuff in my usual spot and looked around. A group of teens walked down the path and it was Eric, Grey, Chris, Missy and Cindy.

"Hey everyone!" I screamed, and ran over. We all hugged and Eric gave me a big, sort of gross wet kiss as we walked to my blanket.

Cindy said, "Look how tanned you are Jez, you look great."

"Thanks, yeah, I've been at the beach a whole lot. I can't believe you're all here!" It felt like such a lot had happened since I'd seen everyone at the bayside party. The familiar sight of my friends made a lump in my throat and tears at the back of my eyes. After hugging everyone a million times, we all spread out on the blankets.

Missy took out her art pad and began sketching everything in sight. Chris and Eric opened beers and talked pre-season football and the Patriots, and Grey put on a Dead tape and asked me if I wanted to make a sand castle.

"Let's make a tennis ball castle," I said.

Ball castles had tunnels and ramps and holes. I always brought a tennis ball in my beach bag for this very purpose. The ball got stuck at the first tunnel so we got back to work and made it smoother, and when the run was perfect, everyone took turns except Missy, who was busy sketching the castle.

Afterwards we ate pretzels and cheese puffs and talked about nothing. No one was in the mood to talk about world events or school or anything of consequence. Cindy started at Ithaca this week, Chris and Eric were going back for their second year at college, Missy and I were seniors, and Grey was working at an alternative school in Watertown. End of summer melancholy, the knowledge that the lazy days of summer would soon be a memory, quieted us.

We stayed on the beach. We stayed when everyone else left. We stayed when it turned dark. We stayed until all snacks were gone and we were hungry. Soon after we trudged back to my house where we all used the bathroom, and changed from our bathing suits.

We sat on my front steps. Missy had her arm around me and Eric held my hand. It felt so great having my friends here and I wanted them to stay forever. "What's next?"

It was eight o'clock and still sticky hot, flies and mosquitoes eating salt off our skin and avoiding our swats. Everyone wanted Antonio's at the arcade for pizza. We piled into Eric's Buick. I sat on Grey's lap in back, purposely not taking the girlfriend seat. Even though Eric had run his hands down my legs a few times at the beach, it was pretty clear we weren't a couple, and even though it felt good and I didn't say stop, I knew I wasn't his anymore.

Antonio's Two had run down booths with cracked leather seats and the best pizza on the South Shore—Antonio's One was in the North End, fancier with the same fantastic food. We got a booth and two large pies, one cheese and one pepperoni. Eric paid for everything saying that his weed business was doing well. The speakers blasted *Layla* by Derek and the Dominos and we sang along in between bites.

The other booths were filled, mostly with teenagers. A bunch of kids walked past our table and a red-haired boy stopped and said, "Hi Jezebel, remember me?" His smile was sardonic and I didn't remember him so I smiled and he left. Perhaps we made-out one summer, he had that look of someone I may have tried for a few days and found boring.

Eric said, "Hi Jezebel, remember me? I'm the one you blew in the sand dunes."

I threw a crust across the table. "Shut up. I don't even know who that was."

Grey took the crust and collected all the others and started making a design. Missy helped him and they made a tic-tac-toe board. We balled up some dough for markers and played for a while until Grey ate the board pieces.

We walked past the arcade and discussed playing skee-ball though no one wanted to. Eric put his arm around me and nibbled on my neck which tickled so I pushed him away. "You look so hot, I bet we get married one day," he said.

I had no reply, didn't intend on getting married one day to him or anyone. We rode back to my house stuffed with pizza, sun-drenched and tired. When the car pulled up outside my house, I kissed everyone goodbye and got out. Eric followed me to the sidewalk. Leaning against his car, he started kissing me passionately, his hands all over my body.

It made me confused, so I pulled away. "Hey, we're friends, okay?"

He tilted his head, examining my face. "Wow, okay. I love you Jez."

"Love you too. Have fun at college."

Waving to the back of his Buick, I watched them ride down the road. That empty feeling, the awful hollowness of being alone I usually got when friends left wasn't there and I felt okay. A loud chorus of August crickets chirped. Stars were bright and the echo of waves crashed against the shore. Soon I was going to leave the beach, soon another change was coming, something beyond all of this, and I was ready.

CHAPTER TWENTY-THREE: SISTERS

The next morning, I woke up wishing it was Monday and my lesson with Sparky. I also had an overwhelming urge to call Quinn. He would be happy that I found Sparky. He would whisper in my ear, *that's great, Jezzy.* I'd hide myself in the warmth of his skin. He'd re-fall in love with me. I'd move into his apartment, play with his band, and everything would be better.

As I put on my bathing suit I realized I had to find the right time to ask Mom for money for my piano lesson. The opportunity came that afternoon.

Mom was at her usual spot on the beach and a big card game was in progress. There were five men and Mom playing. Everyone had drinks in one hand, cards in the other, except the two fat women with big hats who were watching. A pile of money was on our green and yellow striped beach towel. I waited until after a hand was played and as someone shuffled the cards, I walked over.

"I'm going to Boston for the day tomorrow, Mom. I need money."

She smiled and picked a twenty off the pile. "Money? We have plenty!" The men laughed as she waved it in the air.

Barry said, "Your Mom's on a winning streak." He had a big fat cigar at the side of his mouth with drool on it, and everyone was pretty trashed. When Mom handed me the money, I kissed her cheek which surprised her, she glanced at me and her eyes cleared for a minute before shifting back to the game.

I walked back to my blanket. All around me people were involved with end-of-summer activities. It seemed like there was a panic to build another sand castle, dive into one last wave, get that elusive tan or one last ice cream from the ice cream man.

"Jezebel!"

It was Rachel! She waltzed towards me with two friends. They were a vision of elegance, all of them wearing long, sheer beach dresses of pastel colors, their pale skin glowing. A warm breeze blew and it seemed they were floating towards me, the sun a spotlight on their bodies.

"Rachel, you're finally here!" I jumped up, ran over and hugged her. "I missed you so much. I didn't know you were coming today!"

"Missed you so much too, Jez. It was a last-minute thing."

It was so good to see her. Usually she was tan like me but since she had been dancing inside all summer, she had freckles all over her pale skin.

"Meet my friends, Jez. Elizabeth and Miriam."

Elizabeth was tall with brown eyes, dark hair, chiseled face with high cheekbones, model pretty and lanky. Miriam had red-streaked wavy brown hair, a curvy, strong body, grey-green eyes, and was also beautiful. They both smiled with the same full lips.

"It's so great to be outside and this beach is beautiful," Miriam said. She took out a thermos and poured thick, gross greenish liquid into a cup. When she saw the look on my face she laughed. "I'm fighting a cold. This is an herbal mixture, awful tasting, you don't want to know."

I studied Rachel's friends as they spread out towels and opened an umbrella. "You look alike."

"We're sisters," Elizabeth said.

"So are we!"

Rachel tilted her head. "Jez, they know that."

"Oh, yeah. So, how long can you stay?"

Elizabeth stretched her legs in a V-shape on the blanket. "I'm so tight from that marathon rehearsal yesterday."

All three had their toenails painted, Elizabeth pink, Miriam orange and Rachel light green. I was the one on the beach all the time with bare feet, and my toenails were plain, with sand crystals wedged under the nails.

"We can only stay a few hours, there's a concert in Boston tonight. Let's do a walk and talk." Rachel stood and we linked arms, walking towards the water.

Rachel kicked at the surf with a dreamy expression "I miss the beach. Look how pale I am compared to you." We put our arms side by side.

"Yeah, I may have a great tan but it's been such a strange summer, Rachel." Which do I tell her first? Quinn, farm house, Krishnas, John, Sparky? Mom? Fried clams lunch.

"You missed Bubbie's clam lunch. Mom wasn't there either."

"I couldn't. You know I was at dance. Why not Mom?"

A baby sat in a small pool of water holding a yellow plastic shovel. Another baby was near in a similar small pool, crying and pointing to the shovel, as parents stood around snapping pictures of them.

"Mom was with Barry—did you meet him?"

"We stopped for a minute at her card game, which one was he?"

"Too tan, fake smile, fat hard stomach, full head of maybe fake hair, cigar."

She laughed. "I think I met him."

"Mom's been with him all summer."

"What do you mean, *with* him?"

I wished she had seen what I saw. "As if he's her boyfriend, Rachel. Dad's been gone most of the summer, except for July fourth when they had a fight and he left early. And Bubbie's fried clams lunch."

Rachel's expression had changed, some cloud passed over her as if she was annoyed with me. "They're just friends, Jez. You know how Mom is."

"Blue sea glass!" I scooped a piece nestled in the mud. "I've been looking for this all summer."

Smooth corners, transparent middle, different blue shades. My luck was changing! Sparky, Rachel being here, and now, blue sea glass.

But I still needed to tell Rachel. "At Bubbie's clam lunch, Dad acted weird, like he didn't want to be there. Next year I'll just go with Bubbie."

"Jez, stop. I had an internship."

"Okay, sorry. Anyway, we got back and Dad hit me, said I should be more like you."

"What? He hit you?"

"He said I flirted with the waiter which I didn't. Even if I did, what's the big deal? But I didn't."

"He hit you for that?"

Rachel was my only hope with this family and I didn't want her mad, so I said it fast. "Not quite for that. When he said I should be more like you, I told him you were pregnant."

Rachel stopped walking. "What? Why'd you say that?"

"It was infuriating, Rachel, he was picking on me. He didn't believe me anyway, and he smacked me after I said that."

Two guys ran a race into the waves, the first guy yelled, "Victory!"

Rachel shook her head, then started making patterns in the mud with her toes. "That doesn't make sense, Jez. Why did he hit you?"

"I don't know, because he knew I was lying? Or from lunch? I don't know."

Rachel's eyes glazed over. "Certain things about Mom and Dad you have to ignore."

"He smacked me hard! I can't ignore that."

Her feet moved, small dance steps. "Other stuff, I mean."

I kicked at a shell, turned it over with my toe, and decided to leave it nestled with its friends.

"I can't ignore anything, Rachel, it's not who I am. Even my name Jezebel. It stands for courage, truth, being outspoken. I met a lot of wise and cool people this summer, Rachel. They said I was a truth-seeker. They said I'm spiritual, powerful. I learned to take pause, be contained. Arjuna said life was a battlefield, an inner and outer fight for our virtues."

Rachel stopped and raised her eyebrows, a slight grin on her face. "I have no idea what you just said."

I was about to explain about inner feelings and insights, tell her about Quinn, when her friends came sashaying over, their cover-ups making silhouettes of their languid movements as they twirled together into the ocean.

"There's so much more to tell you, Rachel, can't you stay?"

"After next week's performance I'll be home, packing for college. We can hang out; you can help me get ready."

"Don't leave me! Please let me live in your dorm room."

Rachel laughed and didn't realize I wasn't kidding. She had to know how hard it would be, me alone with our parents.

Sitting by the shore, letting the cool water roll over my legs, I studied the piece of sea glass as Rachel and her friends waded and splashed, knee-high in the water. The glass was smooth, oval shaped. It almost made me feel better but not really.

The haze of the August sun was low in the sky. Seagulls circled, waves crashed.

I held Rachel's hand as we walked back to our towels. "Please stay tonight?"

"We can't, Jez, we're meeting friends from our dance program."

They started packing up their stuff and I felt desperate—we hadn't even really talked about anything.

"Rach, I forgot to tell you, I'm going to Berklee School of Music on Monday for a jazz piano lesson!" I started talking fast. "Don't tell Mom, she'll just get weird. It's with this woman Sparky, who I thought was a man. I've been searching all summer for her. Can you believe it? That's one of the great things that happened, also I had a boyfriend, a musician, and…other stuff."

All three were looking at me and I felt like a pariah.

Rachel gave me a hug. "That's great, Jez, I can totally see you playing jazz. Look, we'll talk more soon. You'll be at the performance and after that, we can sit down and you can tell me everything."

It was sad to see them go. But I knew that Monday would be here soon and I would have my first lesson with Sparky. And I found the blue sea glass, which would be my lucky charm.

I fell asleep on my blanket and woke to an empty beach, night beginning to fall. The stars came out, bright in the expanse of the dark sky. Even though this summer had been lonely and scary, wise, new people were in my life now. Opportunities. Meeting John and his brother at this very spot. John saying I was smart, creative, beautiful.

Arjuna's smile, his bright blue eyes, calling me strongly spiritual, a truth seeker. Stephanie in her orange robe, knit hat, sweet voice.

Quinn and the jazz world he invited me into. The intimate times we had, his love, our sad goodbye. My wish for later, some day.

And things inside myself that illuminated, things that no one could take from me.

CHAPTER TWENTY-FOUR: SPARKY

It was Monday, August 26, and summer was rolling to a close on another hot, sunny day. At the 10:55 ferry, I watched people exit with their beach bags, hurrying to enjoy the last days of summer. My green sundress was clean and only a bit wrinkled, my skin tanned and moisturized, my hair brushed neatly. I hoped my appearance said, serious piano student.

In my batik bag was a Duke Ellington song book, a pad of paper for notes, my sweater, and some red hots and grape gum, the last bits of my penny candy. A swift ride later we docked at the wharf. I was early so I decided to walk to Berklee.

Curious what Sparky would teach me I window-shopped music stores and counted the minutes until my lesson. Finally, it was ten minutes of one and I walked through Berklee's front door and upstairs to the second floor. It felt like ages since I had been here though it was only two months ago, at Quinn's rehearsal. Sweet memories surged through me—the music, his apartment, his love. The possibility of running into him here made my heart pound even faster than it already was.

Sounds of piano, flute, and someone vocalizing came from closed doors. I felt nervous, excited, my stomach in knots. I peeked into an open door and there was a woman standing by an upright piano. Her head was bent as she looked through some papers. Tall, with wavy hair, full lips painted red, she wore a jean mini-skirt, red platform sandals, and a tight, yellow tee-shirt.

"Hello?"

When she saw me, her eyes brightened. "Jezebel."

I walked in. "Hi, you must be Sparky, Ana, I mean, Miss Rodriquez?"

"Sparky is fine, after all, that's how you heard about me." Her voice was a low, sexy alto. "Look at you, how pretty, and what a nice tan. You must have been at the beach."

I nodded and smiled, staring at her, then looked quickly away, not wanting to appear too eager.

"Okay, Jezebel, let's get started."

Sparky led me over to the piano and asked about my history with lessons. She had me sight read a simple version of *Hey Jude*, and had me play some basic scales. The keys were smooth beneath my fingers which I remembered to curl, and sit up straight, playing with a loose wrist. When the song was over I folded my hands, making a mental note to cut my fingernails and get the dirt out from under them, maybe paint them red like Sparky's.

"Jezebel, you have a lot of feeling in those fingers."

Not sure if that was a compliment, I nodded. Sparky showed me some basic chords and as she wrote them on an empty music sheet, said she'd teach me chord structure, then more complicated combinations including improvisation.

"The song I'll give you this week is simple and will help you get used to playing the chords we just went over. I'll play it for you to give you an idea of what the sound and tempo should be." She sat beside me, smelling like a mixture of flowers and vanilla.

The song was *Georgia On My Mind*. I watched her hands move over the keys and listened as her husky voice sang.

The second time Sparky played the song she counted beats with a soft 'da, da, da', demonstrating the tempo. "Beautiful song, isn't it? Stuart Gorrell and Hoagy Carmichael. Of course, Billie Holiday mastered it, and Ray Charles also rocked it."

Wishing I had something smart to say, I just nodded, and made a mental note of all the musicians she named so I could research them.

Sparky took out her appointment book. "Darling, our next lesson has to be in two weeks due to Labor Day, so, Monday, September 9th at 3:30?"

"Yes, that's great!"

She took my hand and smiled. "Jezebel, you have a smooth touch with the keys and I can tell you're a fast learner. We'll have fun together."

"Thanks so much, I'm really excited about this. Oh, hang on a sec." I dug in my bag and handed her the twenty.

When she gave me five back she smiled. "Make sure you practice!"

My mind worked quickly. Leave beach Tuesday, September 3. Practice hard for the next six days back in Newton. Meet back here Monday, September 9. "Yes, I definitely will."

Sparky walked me to the door. "See you in a couple of weeks!"

I waved and ran down the stairs. On the sidewalk, I kept running, all the way to Boston Common. Thoughts exploded like fireworks: Sparky said I have a smooth touch with the keys! I'm a fast learner! There's a lot of feeling in my hands!

Out of breath, I sat on a bench by the fountain. This was happening, my dream was coming true!

The urge to tell someone, someone who would be happy for me, overwhelmed me. Who? Quinn might be on the road, and might not be thrilled if I called. John would be happy, but he was probably in class.

Bubbie.

I walked across the street to a pay phone.

She picked up on the tenth ring when I was just about to hang up. "Hello?"

"Hi Bubbie, it's Jezebel."

"Speak up, I can't hear you."

I yelled into the phone, "Bubbie, it's Jezebel, can I come visit?"

"When, when will you come?"

"In about twenty minutes," I hollered.

"I'll be in the garden," she hollered back.

Six stops on the T and I was at her building, walking around back. The garden was filled with bright colored flowers, evenly planted trees, and a small meadow of green grass centered in the courtyard. There were benches that had golden plaques with names of dead people. Emma 'Babs' Goldstone, from her loving children, Roy 'Lefty' Cohen. Many people were around, holding onto the arms of their friends or relatives as they strolled a slow, easy pace. I found Bubbie sitting on a bench, talking with another woman, her long, black-grey hair braided. She wore a thin, faded cotton dress, the buttons taut against her thick bust and waist.

When she spotted me, her face lit up. "This is my granddaughter, come here, bubeleh." I leaned over and she kissed my cheek, then faced her friend. "You can go now." The lady didn't seem upset by her bluntness; she must have known that's just the way Bubbie was.

I sat, and Bubbie pushed my hair behind my ears. "You have such a pretty face; you should wear your hair back." Her brown eyes were soft and clear, and she looked at me with care. "Look how tan and shapely you are." She put her hands on my waist and squeezed, and I felt myself blushing.

"Thanks, Bubbie, I swim and bike a lot."

"Do you have a boyfriend? You had a dark-haired boy, Aaron, a nice Jewish boy."

She meant Eric, and if I was truthful I'd say he wasn't that nice, but I just said he was at college so we weren't together. She took my hand, hers so white compared with mine, with deep wrinkles, wide strong fingers.

"Bubbie, did you ever play an instrument?"

Patting my hand, she just smiled, so I continued. "Today was my first jazz piano lesson, Bubbie. The teacher said I was talented."

"Of course you're talented. Your mother used to play piano, how is Sylvia?"

How is my mom, well, great, Bubbie, she spent the whole summer with a guy that's not your son, she has no idea what's happening with me, and she threatened to stay at the beach house. What I really said was, "Fine, she's fine." And then I changed the subject.

"Bubbie, I started to meditate this summer, have you ever done that, sit cross-legged, close your eyes, watch your breath and get calm. It's helpful, Bubbie. I've had a weird summer—you won't believe some of the things that happened."

She watched people walk by and I didn't know if she was listening, still I kept going. "Two weird things happened with guys, Bubbie. It was really scary." Pausing, I wondered how much to tell. "This last time, I pushed the guy and he fell into a bonfire and got hurt—Bubbie, it was self-defense, he was a creep. I didn't plan on pushing him."

"Did this man hurt you?" Bubbie squeezed my hand and her smile disappeared. I shook my head. "He could have hurt you. You have to be more careful, Bubelah, who's watching you?"

Not knowing what to say, I stayed silent. If Bubbie knew about the farmhouse guy she would have flipped, that image was still stuck in a corner of my mind, hidden yet not forgotten, intense. She perused the garden and was quiet except for clicking her false teeth. There was a yellow flower bush with all these monarch butterflies that zipped around, landed to drink nectar, flitted away. Beautiful.

"In a year you'll be in college, responsible for yourself, you'll be more careful." In her lap Bubbie had a beaded purse which she reached for. Unsnapping the clasp, she took out a faded black and white photo. Bubbie was sitting on a couch with two other women. She was a younger version of herself with the same long hair, thick round face and strong build. The woman in the middle was holding up a magazine or newspaper, it was hard to see because of how faded the picture was.

She pointed. "Sonia Freedmeyer, vice president of the Dorchester socialist party. I was secretary, Mert over here was treasurer. My best friends."

"You were a feminist, Bubbie!"

"Feminist, schmeminist. We were poor. We fought for people's rights. In 1942, when this picture was taken, the FBI agents knocked on my apartment door on Blue Hill Avenue. We had the meetings in my apartment."

"Did they arrest you?"

She laughed which turned into a low cough. I patted her back. "No, it was to scare us. I told them to leave us innocent people alone and go chase the real criminals. They left, never came back, just wrote our names on the list." Bubbie put the picture back, took out a tissue and blew her nose. "Always be strong, Jezebel. They will call you bossy. Don't let that stop you. You defend yourself and help others, especially the disadvantaged. Stand up for your beliefs." She patted my cheek. "Come, we'll have a glass of tea."

Her pace was slow, footsteps heavy, four floors up. Bubbie's strength, her fierceness, reminded me of parts of myself that were uncovered this summer, the Queen Jezebel parts.

As Bubbie put on the kettle in her kitchen, I looked around. The air smelled like forgotten food, like when you don't brush your teeth for a few days and there's food left in the spaces. I opened a window and pictured living here with Bubbie. I'd come home early after school, help grocery shop, make sure her windows were open.

A few oranges and a container of green thick soup were the only items in her refrigerator. "Bubbie, you don't have milk."

She waved her hand in the air. "Eh, I need to shop, we'll do without."

Somehow, Bubbie got her groceries up four flights. It seemed arduous, though. It was obvious she needed help, perhaps a live-in, like a granddaughter who was looking for escape. There was an extra bedroom, the small one in back with the old, faded green bedspread and beat-up dresser, faded flowered curtains covering two windows that looked out to the garden. It could be my own room, which I never had.

We sat on the sofa with our tea, and I tried to get more information about her political activity, except she was done talking. I hoped she'd tell me about Dad, his personality as a kid, so I could understand where everything turned ugly for him. Or maybe I didn't want to know.

With a shawl over her shoulders, Bubbie rested, nodding into her afternoon nap. There was a historical feeling about her, and I was proud we had the same blood, that fight-back survivor's blood that pulsed though her thick face, her constitution. If I lived with Bubbie, she would tell me more stories. I'd make an oral history as a project. That's what I'd tell Mom so she'd let me stay. Bubbie was a project.

I whispered goodbye, ran to T, and soon was on the ferry back home. This time I sat up top and let the wind blow though my hair, the ocean spray cool. There was new sheet music in my bag, I had found my jazz piano teacher and it was the one and only Sparky!

Thirty minutes later I was on my bike riding home, my pace slow. Next summer was before I'd go to college and who knows where I would be. On tour with Quinn and his band. Taking care of Bubbie. Anything felt possible.

Daylight faded. Back towards Boston the sky was magnificent, full of orange glow, red haze with a golden hue, and people sat atop the wall by the yacht club, taking pictures as they watched the sunset. Seagulls swooped into the bay. As the sun dipped below the horizon, people on the wall clapped, and I did too. At the magic house shadows danced along the painted rocks. Dusk settled as I continued my easy ride home, hungry and imagining a full refrigerator, since I hadn't eaten since this morning.

Mom's car was on the street and I put my bike away, entering the dark house, turning on lights.

"Hello?" If Mom was here with Barry that would be gross. Mom's bedroom was empty, perfectly neat, my room was perfectly a mess, so everything was normal. In the refrigerator, there was a white paper bag with cooked lobster and shrimp, someone's leftovers, probably Mom's since she was less than a nibbler and there was a lot left.

I made a platter of the seafood and melted some butter, sat at the table and covered a fat, pink chunk of lobster with steaming, hot butter which tasted amazing. After finishing the food, I pushed the plate away and sat still, my gaze towards the front yard. It was dark, quiet.

What to do next? There were college catalogs I hadn't even opened in my room, books to read, music to learn. Sweet sleep underneath clean sheets. A pile of mail by the couch caught my eye, a small orange envelope on top with a thicker brown envelope underneath. They were both addressed to me, and I grabbed them and went to my room.

My name was type written on the orange envelope, no return address, and I ripped it open to find a card with a picture of the Dalai Lama smiling at me. On the back was written, in bold letters, a quote by him: "Truth is the only weapon we possess."

The card smelled like incense. A lotus flower was above the words and I stared at it for a while. It was an answer to my plea for help, and I read the card again. "Truth is the only weapon we possess."

All these summer days, that was the message that pulsed somewhere in me, and now my answer was unlocked, given, as this gift. Bubbie had said it, Arjuna told me, John encouraged it. And that's what my namesake Queen Jezebel represented. Speaking the truth. Like I had done with Mom and Rachel. Say the truth, even if no one believes me.

As I stared at the card I remembered there was another envelope. This one was handwritten, addressed to 'Miss Jezebel Berke' with a Cambridge return address. I tore the brown paper off and found a book, *High Priest*, by Dr. Timothy Leary. No note, letter, just this book.

The table of contents showed chapters on faith, mystical experiences, the mind, philosophy, divinity, politics, truth. Also, mushrooms, LSD, sex, Mexico, Allen Ginsberg, poetry.

Both gifts were answers to my letters. Someone had heard me, someone had cared. Gratitude and amazement washed over me.

I turned on my side and held the book and card to my chest. It was so quiet outside. No more of the random July firecrackers, no music blasted from college kids parties, even the wind was still. I listened for the fog horn, hoping for its familiar sound. Mom was probably playing cards on a nearby porch, laughing, her girlish voice a song of summer, the tinkling of ice cubes her percussion. Waves crashed, crickets chirped as they sang their love song to the end of summer, vibrations everywhere. I listened through the wind, heard bells from the Hare Krishnas, their voices chanting joyfully, inspirational words from Arjuna. John's voice, smart and filled with care, Bubbie's strong, clear voice, Quinn's sweet hum, his harmonica. The soulful tune from the alley that night, rescuing me. My new teacher Sparky, her husky voice, piano keys. All this music, connected, everything I heard whether I wanted to or not. The spark of a fire, a siren, a melody. A lullaby, the orchestra, the never-ending song, my own breath.

Turning off the light I put my new book and card under the pillow.

"I had a really good day," I said out loud to no one.

And someone inside of me said, "Yes, you did."

EPILOGUE

It was October, my senior year. My back pack was heavy but my class load was light, with three great electives—playwriting, photography and religion. And piano lessons once a week with Sparky.

Crisp, autumn air blew through the kitchen window as I poured myself a glass of milk. Today was my sixth piano lesson and I was excited to show Sparky my progress. I'd been practicing during my free periods in the music room at school. After my lessons at Berklee, I'd sneak upstairs and peek in the rehearsal room. Still, no sign of Quinn. I didn't give up hope that one of these days I would run into him. I pictured playing him a song and he'd be impressed and beg me to be his girlfriend again.

Bubbie shuffled into the kitchen and moved my hair behind my ears. "Such a pretty face, don't cover it with your hair." I put the kettle on for her and grabbed some sugar cookies from her now well-stocked cabinet.

"I have a piano lesson today, Bubbie."

Her wide face lit up. "My granddaughter, playing jazz. I'll come to your recital."

No reason to tell her there probably wouldn't be a recital, like in grade school. Bubbie pointed to a drawer next to the refrigerator.

"Take the money to pay your teacher, Bubelah, take extra for the train." I knew Dad was giving her more money since I had moved in, and Bubbie was generous. Dad seemed to appreciate me being there, but Mom was so mad, she'd barely spoken with me since September.

It was after Rachel's dance concert when she hadn't left for college yet that I told them I wanted to live with Bubbie for a while. I had lit a candle to Queen Jezebel, channeled her strength and caught my parents when they were in the kitchen. It was lunchtime and Dad was eating a fried bologna sandwich on rye.

"Bubbie needs my help. She can barely walk up the stairs, never mind carry groceries. And besides, I want to do an oral history of her, complete with pictures." Which would only take a few afternoons but I didn't say that. "Mom, it will help her, and I want a change."

Mom didn't understand. "You live here, this is your home." What I didn't say was, no Mom, I don't feel safe here, Rachel will be gone and I can't be here anymore.

"It will be a trial, Mom. Just until Thanksgiving. And we can meet in Harvard Square for lunch." Those were happy times with Mom, since she loved the cafes almost as much as the beach. The thought that maybe we could get close again and I could really talk with her when she was relaxed with a strong cup of tea and some sweets gave me hope.

The day I moved in, Bubbie was so happy she took me around her neighborhood, introducing me to all the shop keepers. "My granddaughter." Really embarrassing. We walked past a multi-service counseling center and I peeked in the window.

"That's for troubled people, you don't need that," Bubbie had said.

One of these days I planned to stop in and follow Dear Abby's advice. I'd tell someone everything that was tucked away in a corner of my mind. The stuff that made me sit up panicked in the middle of the night, hands sweaty, breath in my throat.

"Put the money in this envelope so you don't lose it," Bubbie said now, handing me a white envelope as I went to the spare room to get a sweatshirt. She had put up a mirror that leaned against the dresser, it was big with an old wooden frame. In the frame, I had stuck my pictures. A black and white of Bubbie by her first car, Rachel and I in our bathing suits at the beach, Nina Simone at her piano, the Dalai Lama's card, and a beautiful picture I found in Harvard Square of Queen Jezebel. She was wearing a crown, her eyes sparkled, and her full lips were painted red. She was powerful. Alluring. Challenging.

On my way out, I kissed Bubbie on her cheek. "See you after my lesson."

Four flights down to the sidewalk, I was greeted by a bright day with a cool wind. The perfect day to learn a new song, the perfect day for music.

And a perfect day to mail my last letter.

October, 1974

Dear Dad,

This letter is about things that are really hard to talk about, so I'm writing you while living with Bubbie who I love, and thanks for making Mom say yes.

When you showed me Playboy that day and talked about my bras, that felt really awful and uncomfortable. When you look at my body it feels like you're looking at me not like a Dad should. And when I sat with you on the couch and you touched me…that was so creepy and I don't know if it was a mistake but it can't ever ever happen again.

I met a lot of wise people last summer, Dad, good people. They all advised me to speak up, be strong, and seek the truth. And Bubbie spoke the truth too, right? Like with the FBI in the McCarthy era?

Please don't be mad and please change the way you are with me, Dad.

I love you and need you.

Love, Jezebel

At the corner of the street, I paused before I stuck the letter in the large blue mailbox. On the screen of my mind was the picture of Queen Jezebel with her blazing eyes. *We got this, Jez,* she said. I said.

The trolley was pulling up. I stuck the letter in the box and started running.

Acknowledgments

Gratitude to my writer friends for their love, encouragement and feedback: Linda Kelly, Karen, Lisa, David Brunetti, C.J., Susan, Rebecca, Shanti, Nano. To my smart and awesome editor, Ammi Keller, to the Writer's Hotel Shana and Scott for encouraging this novel from the start, to Baz for making my book beautiful, to SCBWI, and to my sons, Miles and Casey, who continue to cheer me on as a writer and author.

Lesley Meirovitz Waite is the author of the Young Adult novel *Walking On Train Tracks*. She lives and writes in NYC and by the beach in Massachusetts.
Visit her online @ lesleymwaite.com

Made in the USA
Columbia, SC
26 August 2024

40730367R00121